The Hill Bachelors

VIKING

75 years

By the Same Author

The Hill Bachelors

WILLIAM TREVOR

VIKING

FIC
TRE

VIKING
Published by the Penguin Group
Penguin Putnam Inc., 375 Hudson Street,
New York, New York 10014, U.S.A.
Penguin Books Ltd, 27 Wrights Lane, London W8 5TZ, England
Penguin Books Australia Ltd, Ringwood, Victoria, Australia
Penguin Books Canada Ltd, 10 Alcorn Avenue,
Toronto, Ontario, Canada M4V 3B2
Penguin Books (N.Z.) Ltd, 182-190 Wairau Road,
Auckland 10, New Zealand

Penguin Books Ltd, Registered Offices:
Harmondsworth, Middlesex, England

First published in 2000 by Viking Penguin,
a member of Penguin Putnam Inc.

1 3 5 7 9 10 8 6 4 2

"Three People" first appeared in *London Magazine*; "Of the Cloth," "The Mourning,"
"A Friend in the Trade," "The Telephone Game," and "The Hill Bachelors" in *The New
Yorker*; "Good News" in The Hudson Review; "The Virgin's Gift" in *The Sunday Times*
(London); and "Against the Odds" in Harper's Magazine. "Le Visiteur" (under the title
"The Summer Visitor"), "Death of a Professor," and "The Telephone Game" were
published in Great Britain in individual volumes by Travelman Publishing, Colophon
Press, and Waterstone, respectively.

PUBLISHER'S NOTE
These selections are works of fiction. Names, characters, places, and incidents either
are the product of the author's imagination or are used fictitiously, and any resemblance
to actual persons, living or dead, business establishments, events, or locales is entirely
coincidental.

LIBRARY OF CONGRESS CATALOGING IN PUBLICATION DATA
Trevor, William, 1928-
The hill bachelors / William Trevor.
p. cm.
ISBN 0-670-89373-0
I. Title.
PR6070.R4 H55 2000
823'.914—dc21   00–032485

This book is printed on acid-free paper.

Printed in the United States of America
Set in MT Baskerville

Contents

Three People

On the steps of the Scheles' house, stained glass on either side of the brown front door, Sidney shakes the rain from his plastic mackintosh, taking it off to do so. He lets himself into the small porch, pauses for a moment to wipe the rain from his face with a handkerchief, then rings the bell of the inner door. It is how they like it, his admission with a key to the porch, then this declaration of his presence. They'll know who it is: no one else rings that inner bell.

'Good afternoon, Sidney,' Vera greets him when the bolts are drawn back and the key turned in the deadlock. 'Is still raining, Sidney?'

'Yes. Getting heavy now.'

'We did not look out.'

The light is on in the hall, as it always is except in high summer.

Sidney waits while the bolts are shot into place again, the key in the deadlock turned. Then he hangs his colourless plastic coat on the hall-stand pegs.

'Well, there the bathroom is,' Vera says. 'All ready.'

'Your father –'

'Oh, he's well, Sidney. Father is resting now. You know: the afternoon.'

1

'I'd hoped to come this morning.'

'He hoped you would, Sidney. At eleven maybe.'

'The morning was difficult today.'

'Oh, I don't mind, myself.'

In the bathroom the paint tins and brushes and a roller have been laid out, the bath and washbasin covered with old curtains. There is Polyfilla and white spirit, which last week Sidney said he'd need. He should have said Polyclens, he realizes now, instead of the white spirit; better for washing out the brushes.

'You'd like some tea now, Sidney?' Vera offers. 'You'd like a cup before you begin?'

Vera has sharp cheek-bones and hair dyed black because it's greying. The leanness in her face is everywhere else too; a navy-blue skirt is tight on bony hips, her plain red jumper is as skimpy as a child's, clinging to breasts that hardly show. Her large brown eyes and sensuous lips are what you notice, the eyes expressionless, the lips perhaps a trick of nature, for in other ways Vera does not seem sensuous in the least.

'Tea later.' Sidney hesitates, glancing at Vera, as if fearing to offend her. 'If that's all right?'

And Vera smiles and says of course it's all right. There is a Danish pastry, she says, an apricot Danish pastry, bought yesterday so she'll heat it up.

'Thanks, Vera.'

'There's Father, waking now.'

Lace Cap is the colour chosen. Sidney pours it into the roller dish and rolls it on to the ceiling, beginning at the centre, which a paint-shop man advised him once was the best way to go about it. The colour seems white but he knows it isn't. It will dry out a shade darker. A satin finish, suitable for a bathroom.

'The tiling,' Mr Schele says in the doorway when Sidney has already begun on the walls. 'Maybe the tiling.'

Clearing away his things – his toothbrush and his razor – Mr Schele noticed the tiling around the washbasin and the bath. In places the tiling is not good, he says. In places the tiles are perhaps a little loose, and a few are cracked. You hardly notice, but they are cracked when you look slowly, taking time to look. And the rubber filler around the bath is discoloured. Grubby, Mr Schele says.

'Yes, I'll do all that.'

'Not the tiling before the paint, heh? Not finish the tiling first maybe?'

Sidney knows the old man is right. The tile replacement and the rubber should be done first because of the mess. That is the usual way. Not that Sidney is an expert, not that he decorates many bathrooms, but it stands to reason.

'It'll be all right, Mr Schele. The tiling's not much, two or three to put in.'

While the undercoat on the woodwork is drying he'll slip the new tiles in. He'll cut away the rubber and squeeze in more of it, a tricky business, which he doesn't like. He has done it only once before, behind the sink in the kitchen. While it's settling he'll gloss the woodwork.

'You're a good man, Sidney.'

He works all afternoon. When Vera brings the Danish pastry and tea, and two different kinds of biscuits, she doesn't linger because he's busy. Sidney isn't paid for what he does, as he is for all his other work – the club, delivering the leaflets or handing them out on the street, depending on what's required. He manages on what he gets; he doesn't need much because there is no rent to pay. Just enough for food, and the gas he cooks it on. The electricity he doesn't have to pay for; clothes come from the charity shop.

They let him live above the club because there's a room. At night he takes the ticket money, protected in his kiosk by Alfie and Harry at the door; in the daytime he cleans up after the night before and takes the phone messages. All the club's facilities are his to make use of, which he appreciates. Sidney is thirty-four now, thirty-four and one week and two days. He had just turned twenty when he first helped Vera.

In Mr Schele's house they do not ever mention that. They do not talk about a time that was distressing for Vera, and for Mr Schele too. But when Sidney's not in the house, when he's private and on his own, in his room above the club, he talks to himself about it. 'Shining armour,' he repeats because it said that in the paper; still says it if he wants to look. *Knight in Shining Armour*, all across the page. Sometimes, when he's trying to get to sleep, he lies there polishing the armour, laying all the pieces out, unfolding cloths, setting out the Duraglit and the Goddard's.

'Sidney, you stay with us for supper tonight?' There is enough, Vera assures him. Another cup of rice will make it enough, and she recites this Saturday's menu: chicken cooked her way and her good salad, strudel and just a little cream. Then *Casualty* on the TV, five past eight.

4

It is a plea, occasionally made when Sidney is in the house as late as this. Vera begs for company with her invitation, Sidney finds himself reflecting; for another presence besides her elderly father. Vera would have been glad when he didn't come in the morning because he'd have finished earlier, too long before supper, and staying to lunch is never the same.

'I should be getting on.'

'Oh, do stay with us.'

And Sidney does. He sits with Mr Schele in the sitting-room and there's an appetizer, salty little pretzels Vera has bought. No drink accompanies these. Mr Schele talks about his childhood.

'The big rosebush has blown down,' Sidney interrupts, standing by the window now. 'This wind has taken it.'

Mr Schele comes to look and sorrowfully shakes his head. 'Maybe the roots are holding,' he suggests. 'Maybe a little can be done.'

Sidney goes through the kitchen to the garden. 'No,' he says when they all three sit down to eat: the roots have snapped in the fall. The news upsets Mr Schele, who remembers the rose being planted, when Vera was a child. He'll not see another rose grown to that size in the garden, he predicts. He blames himself, but Vera says no and Sidney points out that even roses come to an end.

A strudel enriched with sultanas follows the chicken cooked Vera's way and her good salad, and then they stand in the bathroom doorway, surveying Sidney's work. The bathroom is as new, Mr Schele says, greatly cheered by the sight of it. It is the bathroom as it was the day the house was built.

Everything except the linoleum on the floor, which has been there since 1951, Mr Schele calculates.

'A nice new vinyl,' Mr Schele suggests, and Vera adds that not much is necessary. Two metres and three-quarters, a metre wide: she measured it this morning. 'You lay it down, Sidney?' Mr Schele enquires. 'You lay it for us?'

They know he will. If Vera chooses what she wants and brings the piece back to the house he'll lay it. There is adhesive left over from the time he laid the surround in Mr Schele's small bedroom. In windy weather draughts came up through the cracks between the floorboards, the bedroom being on the ground floor. There's been no trouble since Sidney cut out the vinyl surround and stuck it down, except that Mr Schele still can't get used to the colour, shades of marbled orange.

'For a bathroom,' he states his preference now, 'we keep to pale, heh?'

To go with the Lace Cap, Vera agrees. Maybe even white, to go with the bath and washbasin and the tiles. A flush of pink has crept into Vera's hollow cheeks, and Sidney – knowing Vera well – knows it is there in anticipation of the treat that lies ahead: choosing the floor material, the right weight for bathroom use, a shade to match the paint or the porcelain.

'You can wait another minute, Sidney?' Vera says, and briefly goes away, returning with a piece of card she has torn from a cornflakes packet. 'You brush the paint on that for me, Sidney?' she requests, and Sidney does so and washes out the brush again. His Stanley knife slipped when he was cutting the orange vinyl for the bedroom; he had to have three stitches and a tetanus injection.

'Time for the hospital programme,' Mr Schele reminds Vera, who's disappointed when Sidney shakes his head. Not this Saturday, he explains, because he's on early turn at the club.

'You're good to come, Sidney,' Vera says in the porch, whispering as she always does when she says that. She's older than Sidney, forty-one; she was twenty-seven when he first helped her, the time of her distress.

'It's nothing,' he says before he leaves, his unchanging valediction.

*

They took Vera in because in the end they didn't believe her story about an intruder while she was at the cinema. They had accepted it at first, when everything hung together – the kitchen window forced open, the traces of dry mud on the draining-board and again by the door, where the shoes had been taken off. Forty-eight pounds and ninepence had been taken, and medals and a silver-plated stud-box. The hall door and the porch door were both wide open when Vera returned to the house; Mr Schele, employed in those days in a radio and television shop, was still at work. They took Vera in because there was something that didn't seem right to them about the entry through the kitchen window, no sign on the path outside of the dried mud, no sign of it on the window-sill. There was something not quite right about only a stud-box and medals taken, not other small objects that were lying about; and no one could remember Vera at the cinema. Then, in the garden, a dog sniffed out part of a glove that had been burnt on the garden fire, and the wool matched the fibres found in the room upstairs. Odd, it seemed, that gloves had been burnt, even if they were old and done for.

All that passes through Sidney's thoughts, as it usually does when he walks away from the house. He isn't late for his Saturday duties at the club; he doesn't hurry. After an afternoon inside, the air is good. The wind that blew away the rain is noisy in the empty trees, lifts off a dustbin lid and plays with plastic flowerpots in the small front gardens. He'll walk until it rains again, then take a bus.

'Come, Angus! Angus!' a woman calls her dog, a Pomeranian. 'What a wind!' she calls out, going by, and Sidney says what wind indeed. He knows the woman from meeting her and her dog on this particular stretch. Several times a day she's out.

Walking through the ill-lit suburban avenues and crescents, leaves scattered on the pavements or gathered into corners by the wind, Sidney remembers the photograph of Vera, her big lips a little parted, her hair – blonde then – falling almost to her shoulders, her eyes innocent and lovely. She was in custody when he saw the photograph; her solicitors, not she, were appealing for anyone who'd seen her entering or leaving the cinema to come forward.

Sidney passes into streets with closed shops and minimarkets, dentists and chiropodists advertised, the Regina take-away, the Queen's Arms at a corner, Joe Coral's betting shop. Then there is a quiet neighbourhood, the yellow caravan still parked in the garden, the open space that's not quite a park, litter sodden on its single path. The film was *French Connection 2*. He went to see it as soon as he saw the photograph, so that he knew the plot.

On the bus Sidney feels like sleep because last night, being Friday, was one of his late ones. But he doesn't sleep because he hates waking up on a bus. Once he went past his stop and had to pay the extra, but that hasn't happened since. Something wakes him, some worry about having to pay the extra again; one stop before his own he always wakes now, but even so he'd rather not sleep. He closes his eyes though, because he wants to go back in his thoughts, to run it again, to make sure it's all still there: usually after he has been to the Scheles' he does that. 'The ice-cream girl was going round,' he said, and every word was written down. 'The lights were up.'

He needn't have sat next to her but he did, he explained. He wanted to; soon's he saw the hair he wanted to, soon's he looked along the row and saw her lips, moving as it happened, sucking a sweet maybe, or chocolate. 'You make a practice of this, Sidney?' the sergeant asked. Well, once or twice before, he said, a woman he liked the look of.

The bus draws in again, three people get off, two men and a girl, the men much older, as if one of them's her father. 'You're certain, Sidney?' the sergeant pressed him, and he said the ice-cream girl took her time, not that anyone was buying from her, a good five minutes it was the lights were up. And there was afterwards too, of course. No way he wasn't certain, he said. 'Definitely,' he said. 'Oh, yes.' The other man came in then, and asked the same questions all over again. 'You tell us what clothes she was wearing, Sidney? Take your time now, son.' It said in the paper about the clothes, and he remembered because he'd learnt it off.

The club is in darkness when he reaches it, but he turns the lights on as soon as he's inside. He tidied this morning, the time he always tidies. Everything is ready. Alfie and Harry arrive, and he makes them Maxwell House the way they like it, and they sit there, drinking it and smoking. Tomorrow he'll go back, Sidney says to himself, tidy up that rose that's come down.

*

The Sunday bells of a church are sounding for an early service when Vera glances from the kitchen window and there he is, cutting up the big rosebush that the wind brought down. A warmth begins in Vera, spreading from some central part of her to her shoulders and her thighs, tingling in her arms and legs. It is the warmth of Vera's passion, heat in her blood that such an unexpected glimpse always inspires. He came to help yesterday. Why today also? The blown-down rosebush could have waited.

'Sidney's come,' her father says, having looked out too. 'Twenty-five years, that rosebush. High as a tree and now we must begin again.'

'Oh, I'm not sorry it's gone. It darkened the garden. Sidney, you like some coffee?' Vera calls from the back door and Sidney waves and says in a minute.

'Is Sidney wearing the garden gloves?' Mr Schele fusses. 'You need the gloves with a rose.'

'Sidney knows.'

Once, working in the garden, sawing up old planks of wood, he got a splinter under a thumbnail and Vera saw to it: Sidney's hand laid flat on the kitchen worktop, a light brought specially in, a needle sterilized in a match flame, TCP and tweezers. In her night-time fantasies she has comforted Sidney, whispering to him, asking him to talk to her. Sometimes, when he has worked all through a weekend morning, she turns the immersion heater on early in case he'd like to have a bath before he goes. The time he cut his hand she staunched the blood flow with a tourniquet.

'Ready, Sidney,' Vera calls from the back door. 'Coffee.'

Mr Schele senses something in the air. His thoughts reflect Vera's: unsightly though it is, the thicket of twisted branches on the grass could easily have stayed there for a week. It is Sidney's pretext, Mr Schele tells himself; it is a reason to come back so soon. He pours hot milk on to his bran flakes and stirs the mixture with his spoon, softening the flakes because he does not like them crispy. Is this, at last, the Sunday of the proposal? He watches Vera at the stove. She remembers her fluffy slippers and hurries away to change them. The glass disc rattles in the milk saucepan and Mr Schele rises to attend to that. He cannot last for ever; each day, at seventy-eight, is borrowed time. What life is it for a woman alone?

Moving the saucepan to one side of the gas jet, Mr Schele accepts that when he is gone Vera will have no one. Going out with chaps – and there used to be quite a few – has been a thing of the past since the trouble. Vera will be alone for the rest of her days: he understands that, although the subject is never mentioned. He understands that her luck might even change for a while, before some new chap she makes friends with has second thoughts, even though at the time she walked away without a stain. That is how things happen, Mr Schele knows, and knows that Vera has worked it out too. Sidney is different because of coming forward, and in a sense he has been coming forward ever since, as good a friend to Vera as he was at the time, a saviour really: in Mr Schele's opinion that word is not too strong. It took time for the opinion to form, as naturally it would in a father, the circumstances as they were.

'It's good of Sidney. Just because that rose blew down.'

'Yes, it is.'

Vera nods, saying that, lending the words a little emphasis. Her father knows what other people know, no more. He came in at his usual time, just after half past six. He saw the white police cars outside and was in a state before he passed through the porch. 'You sit down now,' she said, and told him, and the policewoman brought him tea. 'It can't be,' he kept saying. Later on, she had kippers to boil in the bag, but they didn't want them. She folded up the wheelchair and put it in the cupboard under the stairs, not wanting to look at it. Best to get it out of the house, she decided when everything quietened down, a month gone by, and they got a fair price for it.

'You take your chances, Vera.'

She knows what he means, but Sidney's not going to propose marriage, this morning or any other time, because marriage isn't on the cards and never has been. The intruder would not have guessed there was anyone in that room because when he'd watched the house he'd only ever seen two people coming and going: the policemen explained all that. An intruder always sussed a place, they explained, he didn't just come barging in. Her father out all day from eight-fifteen on, and the villain would have followed her to the cinema and seen her safely in. Cinemas, funerals, weddings: your house-thief loves all that. 'Oh no, that's crazy,' her father kept muttering when they changed their minds, suddenly taking a different line. He had always thought it was crazy, their groundless probing, as he put it. He had always believed their case would fall to bits because it didn't make sense.

'You know what I'm saying, Vera? You take your chances.'

She nods. Changing her slippers for shoes because Sidney had come, she decided as well to change her drab Sunday skirt for her dog-tooth. She stood in front of the long wardrobe looking-glass the way she used to in the old days. She liked to be smart in the old days and she still does now. Sometimes a man looks at her in a supermarket or on the street. And Sidney does, when he thinks she isn't noticing. She heats the milk again and is ready to make fresh coffee.

'You like an egg, Sidney?' she offers when Sidney comes in. 'Poached egg? Maybe scrambled?'

'No, honestly. Thanks, Vera.' It's too windy to risk burning the rosebush, he says, but he has clipped it up, ready for a calmer day.

There's a leaf in his hair, and Vera draws his attention to it. 'You just sit down.'

'Only a cup of coffee, Vera.'

That morning Sidney woke when it was half past six, the light just beginning. He thought at once about Vera, although it had been a particularly rough night in the club and usually that comes into his mind first thing. Harry and Alfie had had to separate youths who began to fight, one of them with a knife. Later, after two, a girl who was a stranger in the club collapsed. But in spite of the intervention of that excitement, this morning it was Vera he woke up to, her face as it was when her hair was blonde. Fleshy you'd have called her face then, soft was what he'd thought when he first saw the photograph, in the *Evening Standard* someone had left behind in the club. It doesn't matter that Vera is leaner now, it doesn't matter that her hair is different. Vera's the same, no way she isn't.

'Dried out a lovely shade,' Mr Schele says. 'The bathroom.'

'There's half that tin left for touching up.' The coffee cup is warm in Sidney's cold hands. He likes that skirt. He'd like to see it folded on a chair and Vera standing in her slip, her jersey still on. The jersey's buttons are at the top, along one shoulder, four red buttons to match the wool. In the photograph it was a jacket, and white dots on her shirt. A loving sister, the paper said.

'Anything on the News, Sidney?'

He shakes his head, unable to answer the question because this morning he didn't turn the radio on. Some expedition reached a mountain top, Vera says.

'Bad night in the club,' Sidney says, and tells them. He'd had to fish light bulbs and tins out of the toilet when he was

14

closing up, but he doesn't mention that. The girl who'd collapsed was on Ecstasy, the ambulance men said. There is some way they can tell an Ecstasy collapse, now that they've got used to them. Sidney doesn't know what it is.

'Out of control,' Mr Schele comments, hearing that. 'The whole globe out of control.'

'Maybe how they sweat. There's different ways a person sweats, an ambulance man told me. According to what's taken.'

The blow left scarcely a contusion. It was to the neck, the paper said, the side of the neck, no more than a smack. The intruder had lost his head; he'd walked into a room where he wasn't expecting anyone to be, and there was a figure in a wheelchair. He'd have been seen at once, but what he didn't know was that he couldn't ever have been described. Probably he struck the blow to frighten; probably he said if a description was given he'd be back. The room is empty now, even the bed taken away; two years ago Sidney painted out the flowery wallpaper with satin emulsion – Pale Sherbet – the woodwork to match in gloss.

'One thing I hate,' he says, 'is when an ambulance has to come.'

God did not make another man in all His world as gentle: often Vera thinks that, and she thinks it now. His voice was gentle when he said about an ambulance coming to take away the Ecstasy girl, the hands that grasp the coffee cup are gentle. 'Short of a slate or two,' they said when they told her a man had come forward. 'But crystal clear in his statements.'

The first time she saw him in court his shabby jacket

needed a stitch. Yes, what he said was true, she agreed when it was put to her, and was told to speak up.

'You see the world at that club, Sidney,' her father says.

When she walked free, when she came back to the house, her father didn't look at her at first. And when he did she could see him thinking that a man who was a stranger to her, whose face she had not even noticed, had reached out to her in the darkness of a cinema, and that she had acquiesced. With her looks, she could have had anyone: that, too, her father didn't say.

'Yeah, a lot come into the club. Though Monday's always light. Not much doing on a Monday.'

She knew he'd visit. She knew in court, something about him, something about the pity that was in his eyes. Nearly a year went by but still she guessed she'd open the porch door and there he'd be, and then he was. He came when he knew her father would be out at work. He stood there tongue-tied and she said come in. 'I couldn't face him,' her father said when she told him, but in the end he did, so much was owing; and now he waits for a proposal. Step by step, time wore away the prejudice any father would have.

'You try that new biscuit, Sidney.' She pushes the plate towards him and then fills up his coffee cup. Nicer than the ones with the peel in them, she says.

'I met that woman with the dog again. Last night.'

They don't know who the woman is. Must be she lives the other side of the green, her father has said when she was mentioned before. On his own walks he has never run into her, preferring to go the other way.

'You think we put in another rose, Sidney?' her father asks.

'It's empty, the way it is. You'd notice that.'

'I thought it maybe would be.'

Mr Schele goes to see for himself, changing his shoes in the shed by the back door. The first time he faced Sidney he kept looking at his hands, unable to keep his eyes off them. He kept thinking of Vera when she was little, when her mother was alive, Mona already confined. Vera always looked out for him, and ran down the garden path to meet him when he came home, and he lifted her up high, making her laugh, the way poor Mona never could, not all her life. The first time he faced Sidney he had to go out and get some air, had stood where he is standing now, near to where the rosebush was. It wasn't wrong that Vera had left Mona on her own that afternoon. Ever since their mother died he'd kept saying to Vera that she couldn't be a prisoner in the house. One sister should not imprison another, no matter what the circumstances were; that was not ever meant. The shopping had to be done; and no one could begrudge an hour or so in a cinema. And yet, he thought the first day he faced Sidney, why did it have to be the way it was, poor Mona's head fallen sideways as though her neck'd been cracked, while that was happening in the cinema's dark?

'I'm sorry there was that trouble,' Vera says in the kitchen, referring to the fight in the club, and the girl for whom an ambulance had come.

'On a Saturday you expect it.' And Sidney says he doesn't

know why that is. Often on a Thursday or a Friday the club's as full. 'I like a Sunday,' he says, quite suddenly, as if he has for the first time realized that. 'There's church bells somewhere near the club. Well, anyway they carry. Could be a mile off.'

On Sunday evenings Vera goes to church, a Baptist place, but anywhere would do. She says she's sorry when she kneels, and feels the better for saying it in a church, with other people there. And afterwards she wonders what they'd think if they knew, their faces still credulous following their hour of comfort. She makes herself go through it when she's on her knees, not permitting the excuses. She wants to draw attention to how awful it was for so long, ever since their mother died, how awful it would always be, the two of them left together, the washing, the dressing, the lifting from the wheelchair, the feeding, the silent gaze. All that, when praying, Vera resists in her thoughts. 'You want to get turned off?' a boy said once, she heard him in the play yard when she was fourteen. 'You take a look at the sister.' And later, when the wheelchair was still pushed out and about, proposals didn't come. Later still, when there were tears and protestations on the street, the wheelchair was abandoned, not even pushed into the garden, since that caused distress also: Mona was put upstairs. 'Vera, take your friend up,' her father, not realizing, suggested once: an afflicted sister's due to stare at visitors to the house. On her knees – kneeling properly, not just bent forward – Vera makes herself watch the shadow that is herself, the sideways motion of her flattened hand, some kind of snap she felt, the head gone sideways too.

'The wind's dropped down. You stay to lunch, Sidney? You could have your fire, eh?'

In the courtroom people gazed at both of them. Asked again, she agreed again. 'Yes, that is so,' she agreed because a man she didn't know wanted her to say it: that for as long as the film lasted they were lovers.

'I'll have the fire,' he says, and when he moves from the window she sees her father, standing by the empty place where the rosebush was. His belief protects them, gives them their parts, restricts to silence all that there is. When her father goes to his grave, will his ghost come back to tell her his death's the punishment for a bargain struck?

'A loin of lamb,' Vera says, and takes it from the fridge, a net of suet tied in place to make it succulent in the roasting. Parsnips she'll roast too, and potatoes because there's nothing Sidney likes more.

'I left my matches at the club.'

She takes a box from a cupboard, swinging back the door that's on a level with her head, reaching in. *Cook's Matches* the label says. She hands them to him, their fingers do not touch. In the garden her father has not moved, still standing where his rosebush was. He's frail, he suffers from the ailments of the elderly. More often than he used to he speaks of borrowed time.

'I'll get it going now,' Sidney says.

There'll be a funeral, hardly different from her mother's, not like Mona's. Their time is borrowed too, the punishment more terrible because they know it's there: no need for a ghost to spell it out.

She smears oil on the parsnips she has sliced, and coats with flour the potatoes she has already washed and dried. Sidney likes roast potatoes crispy. There is nothing, Vera sometimes thinks, she doesn't know about his likes and dislikes. He'll stand there at the funeral and so will she, other people separating them. The truth restored, but no one else knowing it.

'Colder now,' her father says when he comes in. The wind turned, and left a chill behind when it dropped.

He warms himself by standing close to the gas stove, massaging his fingers. Without his presence, there would be no reason to play those parts; no reason to lose themselves in deception. The darkness of their secrets lit, the love that came for both of them through their pitying of each other: all that might fill the empty upstairs room, and every corner of the house. But Vera knows that, without her father, they would frighten one another.

Of the Cloth

He was out of touch, and often felt it: out of touch with the times and what was happening in them, out of touch with two generations of change, with his own country and what it had become. If he travelled outside Ireland, which he had never done, he knew he would find the same new *mores* everywhere, the different, preferred restrictions by which people now lived their lives; but it was Ireland he thought about, the husk of the old, the seed of the new. And often he wondered what that new would be.

The Rev. Grattan Fitzmaurice, Ennismolach Rectory, his letters were addressed, the nearest town and the county following. His three Church of Ireland parishes, amalgamated over the years, were in a valley of pasture land in the mountains, three small churches marking them, one of them now unattended, each of them remote, as his rectory was, as his life was.

The town that was nearest was thirteen miles away, where the mountain slope became a plain and the river that flowed through the townland of Ennismolach was bridged. The rectory was reached from Doonan crossroads by taking the road to Corlough Gap and turning right three miles farther on at the Shell petrol pump. A few minutes later there was the big Catholic Church of the Holy Assumption, solitary and splendid by the roadside, still seeming new although it had been there for sixty years. Over the brow of the next hill were the gates to Ennismolach Rectory, its long curving avenue years ago returned to grass.

This was granite country and Grattan Fitzmaurice had a look of that grey, unyielding stone, visible even in the pasture land of the valley. Thin, and tall, he belonged to this landscape, had come from it and had chosen to return to it. Celibacy he had chosen also. Families had spread themselves in the vast rectory once upon a time; now there was only the echo of his own footsteps, the latch of the back door when Mrs Bradshaw came in the mornings, the yawning of his retriever, the wireless when he turned it on. Emptily, all sound came twice because an echo added a pretence of more activity than there was, as if in mercy offering companionship.

There was, as well, the company of the past: the family Grattan remembered here was his own, his father the rector of Ennismolach before him, his mother wallpapering the rooms and staining the floorboards to freshen them up, his sisters. The rectory had always been home, a vigour there in his childhood, the expectation that it would continue. Change had come before his birth, and the family was still close to revolution and civil war. The once impregnable estates had fallen back to the clay, their people gone away, burnt-out houses their memorial stones. Rectories escaped because in Ireland men of the cloth would always have a place: as the infant nation was nurtured through the 1930s, it seemed in Ennismolach that ends would forever be made to meet in the lofty rooms, that there would forever be chilblains in winter, cheap cuts from the butcher at Fenit Bridge, the Saturday silence while a sermon was composed. And even as a child Grattan had wanted to follow his father's footsteps in this parish.

His father died in 1957, his mother in that year also. By then the congregation at Ennismolach church had dwindled, the chapel of ease near Fenit Bridge hadn't been made use of for years, and melancholy characterized other far-flung parishes in the county. The big houses, which had supported them, tumbled further into ruin; the families who had fled did not return; and from farm and fields, from townlands everywhere, emigration took a toll. 'It'll get worse,' Grattan's father said a few weeks before he died. 'You realize it'll get worse?' It wasn't unexpected, he said, that the upheaval should bring further, quieter upheaval. The designation of the Protestant foundation he served, the 'Church of Ireland', had long ago begun to seem too imposing a title, ludicrous almost in its claim. 'We are a remnant,' Grattan's father said.

It was an irony that they should be, for their Protestant people of the past – Wolfe Tone and Thomas Davis, Emmet and Parnell, the Henry Grattan after whom Grattan was named – had in their different ways and in their different times been the inspiration for the Ireland that had come about, and Grattan knew that its birth was Ireland's due no matter how, in the end, it had happened. Yet it was true: they were a remnant. While Church of Ireland notice-boards still stood by old church gates, gold letters on black giving details of what services could be offered, there was a withering within that Church that seemed a natural thing. Risen from near suppression, the great Church of Rome inherited all Ireland.

In a dream when he was old, Grattan rode on horseback from Ennismolach Rectory, and walked slowly to an altar between crowded pews. The dream came often and he knew it did so because the past was never far from his thoughts. He knew, as well, that the pages could not be turned back, that when the past had been the present it had been uneasy with shortcomings and disappointments, injustice and distress. He did not in any way resent the fact that, while his own small churches fell into disrepair, the wayside Church of the Holy Assumption, with its Virgin's grotto and its slope of new graves, was alive and bustling, that long lines of cars were parked on the verges and in gateways for its Sunday Masses, that there was Father MacPartlan as well as Father Leahy, that large sums were gathered for missions to the African heathen. Father MacPartlan and Father Leahy praised and rejoiced and celebrated, gave absolution, gave thanks. The simplicity of total belief, of belonging and of being in touch, nourished – or so it seemed to Grattan – Father MacPartlan's ruddy features and Father Leahy's untroubled smile.

*

A man called Con Tonan, who had lost the use of an arm in a tractor accident, worked in the garden of Ennismolach Rectory, his disablement rendering him unfit for employment as a farm labourer, which had always been the source of his livelihood. Unable to pay more than a pittance, Grattan took him on when he'd been out of work for a year. Con Tonan, still young then, knew nothing about gardening, but the six-mile bicycle journey to Ennismolach Rectory, and doing what he could to release the choked shrubs and restore the flowerbeds that had all but disappeared, gave a pattern to his day three times a week. Mrs Bradshaw, one of Grattan's flock at Glenoe, began to come to the rectory when Con Tonan was just beginning to understand the garden. Twice a week she drove over from Glenoe in a small, old Volkswagen, a woman who was as warm-hearted as she was dutiful.

That was the household at Ennismolach, Mrs Bradshaw ill-paid also, her arrival on Tuesdays and Thursdays as much an act of charity on her part as the employment of a one-armed man was on Grattan's. Sometimes Con Tonan brought one of his children with him, skilfully balancing the child on the crossbar of his bicycle in spite of the absence of an arm.

For twenty-eight years Con Tonan came to the rectory and then, before one winter began, he decided the journey was too much for him. 'Arrah, I'm too old for it now,' was all he said when he broke the news of his intentions. It was perhaps because his pension had come through, Mrs Bradshaw suggested, but Grattan knew it wasn't. It was because Con Tonan was as old as he was, because he was tired.

Mrs Bradshaw was younger. Plump and respectable, she knew all about the greater world, delighting in its conveniences as much as she deplored its excesses. She and Grattan would sit together at the kitchen table on Tuesdays and Thursdays, exchanging the scraps of news she brought for those he had heard that morning on the radio, which she herself rarely turned on.

He sensed her fondness for him – an old man who was a legend in the neighbourhood simply because he'd been a part of it for so long – and sometimes asked her if it was ever said that he was going on beyond his time. Was it said that he was ineffective in his vocation, that he managed ineffectively what remained of his Church's influence in the amalgamated parishes? He was always reassured. No one wanted him to go, no one wanted some bright young curate to come out from one of the towns on alternate Sundays, to breathe life into what was hardly there.

*

'Mr Fitzmaurice,' a red-cheeked, red-haired youth said, arriving at the rectory on a day in the early summer of 1997. 'My father died.'

Grattan recognized the bicycle the boy dismounted from as the big old Rudge that had once so regularly been pedalled up and down the rectory avenue. He hadn't seen a child of Con Tonan's for years, since one by one they'd all become too heavy to be carried on their father's crossbar.

'Oh, Seamus, I'm sorry. Come in, come in.'

His one-time gardener had died of a stroke, a mercy he hadn't lingered: the boy was articulate, slow but clear in delivering the sombre message.

'He was speechless a day, Mr Fitzmaurice. Then that was the end of it.' His mother had sent him over, and Grattan was touched that he'd been remembered. The funeral was on Monday.

'I'll be there of course, Seamus.'

He made tea and put out biscuits. He asked Seamus if he'd like a boiled egg, but Seamus said no. They talked for a while, until the tea he'd poured was cool and then drunk. Seamus was working for Kelly Bros., who were building two bungalows at Fenit Bridge.

'Are you all right yourself, Mr Fitzmaurice?' he enquired before he mounted the bicycle that now was his. It was serving its third generation, having passed on in the same way to his father.

'Ah, I am, Seamus, I am.'

'I'll be off so.'

Mrs Bradshaw brought the same tidings the next morning. A decent, quiet man, she said, which she had not said in Con Tonan's lifetime. A humble man, who had accepted without bitterness the tragedy that had changed his life. 'Sure, wasn't he happy here?' her comment was, her tone adding one finality to another. She washed their coffee cups at the sink and stacked away the two saucers. She'd brought eggs, she said, the hens beginning to lay again.

On Monday he attended the funeral. He held back afterwards outside the big church that still seemed new, waiting his turn with the widow. He did not know her well; he could remember meeting her only once before, a long time ago.

'He loved going over to the rectory,' she said, and as if something in the clergyman's expression indicated surprise she said it again, her hands grasping one of his. 'Oh, he did, Mr Fitzmaurice, he did,' she insisted. 'It was a good thing in the end, he used say. If he hadn't had the accident he wouldn't have got to know Ennismolach Rectory. He wouldn't have got to know yourself, sir.'

Grattan Fitzmaurice drove away from the funeral, warmed by what had been said to him. Walking with his dog about the garden that had deteriorated in the last few years, although was not as neglected as it had been before he had help in it, he thought about the man who had died, who had become a friend. Con Tonan hadn't known what a daphne was when first he came, nor what choisya and ceanothus were called. He'd been amazed that raspberry canes were cut down to the ground in the autumn. He'd learnt how to rid the roses of suckers and when to clip the yew hedge, and not to burn the leaves that came down in autumn but to let them decay into mould to enrich the soil. The two men had talked about ordinary things: the weather, and sometimes what a new government intended to do, pondering over which promises would be easy to keep, which would have to be abandoned. In other ways they were separated, but that never mattered.

When Grattan had fed his dog on the evening of the funeral, when he'd boiled himself the couple of eggs he always had at a quarter past seven, with toast and a pot of tea, there was the sound of a car. He opened the front door a few minutes later to the younger of the two priests who had conducted the service. Smiling, hand out, Father Leahy said, 'I thought I'd come over.'

He said it easily, as if he were in the habit of calling in regularly at the rectory, as if he knew from long experience that this was a good moment. But neither he nor Father MacPartlan had ever driven up to Ennismolach Rectory before.

'Come in, come in,' Grattan invited. The curate's handshake had been firm, the kind you can feel the friendliness in.

'Isn't that a lovely evening, Mr Fitzmaurice? Are we in for a heatwave?'

'I'd say we might be.'

In the big drawing-room all the furniture was old but not old enough to be valuable: armchairs and a sofa shabby from wear, plant stands and rickety little tables with books and ornaments on them, sun-browned wallpaper cluttered with pictures and photographs, a tarnished looking-glass huge above the white marble mantelpiece, a card-table with a typewriter on it. The long curtains – once two shades of blue – were almost colourless now and in need of repair.

'You'll take a cup of tea, Father?'

'Ah no, no. Thanks though, Mr Fitzmaurice.'

'Well, we've lost poor Con.'

'God rest him.'

'I missed him when coming out here was too much for him in the end.'

Glancing beside him as he sat down, Grattan noticed the *Irish Times*, where earlier he had placed it on the table by his armchair. His eye had been caught then, as it was now, by the grinning countenance of Father Brendan Smyth being taken into custody by a grim-faced detective. *Paedophile Priest is Extradited*, the headline ran. He reached out and turned the newspaper over.

'You'd miss Con, of course.' There was a pause, and then Father Leahy added, 'You're a long way from the world here.'

'I'm used to that.'

He wondered if his gesture with the paper had been noticed. He had meant it as a courtesy, but a courtesy could be offensive. Long way from the world or not, it was impossible not to be aware of the Norbertine priest's twenty-year-long persecution of children in Belfast. One sentence already served in Magilligan Prison in County Derry, he was now on his way to face seventy-four similar charges in Dublin. All day yesterday the News had been full of it.

'It was good of you to attend the funeral, Mr Fitzmaurice.'

'I was fond of Con.'

The funeral service had impressed him. There'd been confidence in its ceremony and its ritual, in the solemn voice of Father MacPartlan, in Father Leahy's, in the responses of the congregation. It was there again in the two priests' gestures, hands raised to give the blessing, in the long line of communicants and the coffin borne away, the graveside exhortations. Founded on a rock, Grattan had thought: you felt that here. The varnished pews were ugly, the figure in the Stations of the Cross lifeless, but still you felt the confidence and the rock.

'Mrs Tonan said the same thing, that it was good of you to come. 'Tis difficult sometimes for a parishioner to understand that someone of your Church would want to.'

'Ah well, of course I would.'

'That's what I'm saying.'

There was a silence. Then Father Leahy said:

'That's a great dog.'

'I'd be lost without Oisín.'

'You always had a dog. I always associate a dog with you in the car.'

'Company.' And Grattan thought you didn't often see a priest with a dog. Maybe once in a while you would, but not often. He didn't say so in case it sounded intrusive. He remembered Father Leahy as a child, one of the Leahys from the white farmhouse on the Ballytoom road. Three brothers he remembered, swinging their legs on a whitewashed wall, waving at him whenever he drove past. The priest would be the youngest, the youngest in all the family, someone told him once. Four girls there were as well.

'We neither of us moved far off,' he said, and Father Leahy nodded, affirming his understanding of how the conversation had drifted in this direction.

'We didn't, right enough,' he said.

Grattan wondered why the curate had come. Had he decided to pay the visit when he saw the lone figure at the funeral? Had he come to offer half an hour of companionship, maybe out of pity? Had the two priests said after the service that perhaps the occasion had been hard to bear for a Protestant clergyman, with nothing of a flock left?

'Your family scattered?' He kept the conversation going, feeling that was required of him.

'Mostly.'

The farm was still run by the brother who'd inherited it, Young Pat. There was another brother in Cleveland, Ohio. The sisters had all gone, married in different parts of the country, two in Cork.

'We used meet up at Christmas, a few of us anyway. They'd come back to the farm, but then the girls have families of their own now. They don't want to be travelling.'

'I remember you sitting on that wall.'

'We used learn off the car numbers. Not that there were many, maybe two a day. ZB 726.'

'Was that my old Morris?'

'The slopey-back green Morris. You used put out one of your indicators when you went by, waving at us. D'you remember that? The little orange yoke?'

'I bought that car from Mr Keane in the Bank of Ireland. Would you have known Mr Keane?'

'I would, of course. Wasn't it Keane himself lent my father the price of the milking parlour? A decent man.'

Protestants were often called decent. You knew where you were with Protestants: that was said often in those days. Straight-dealing was what was meant, the quality not begrudged. The bank manager had been the churchwarden at Ennismolach.

'Father MacPartlan remembers your father. Your mother too.'

Grattan imagined Father MacPartlan mentioning them, telling his curate about the old days, how the big houses had been burnt down, the families driven from them, how the rectories had escaped. 'Wouldn't you call round on the old fellow one of these evenings?' he imagined Father MacPartlan urging. 'If it wouldn't be taken wrong?' And the bluff tones of the older priest continued to disturb Grattan's thoughts, instructing the curate in mercy and understanding, reminding him of the spirit of the different times. After all, it was said also, all three of them shared the cloth.

'Would you care for a stroll in the garden, Father?'

'Well, that would be grand.'

Dusk had settled in. With the dog a few paces behind them, the two men passed from path to path, going slowly, shrubs and flowers pointed out. Father Leahy, like Con Tonan once, knew the names of hardly anything.

'Con knocked the garden into shape for me.'

'His wife was saying you taught him the way of it.'

'Oh, at first of course. He ended knowing more than I did myself. He loved the old garden before he was done with it.'

'He was a long time here.'

'He was.'

'Near enough the time Father MacPartlan entered the priesthood it would have been when he came to you.'

The air was fragrant with the scent of night stock, there was the sound of Oisín rooting in the undergrowth. Rabbits came into the garden, and one scuttled away now.

'Father MacPartlan came off a farm, like I did myself. A lot of priests in Ireland came off a farm.'

'They still do, I'm told.'

'Simple enough lads at first.'

'Yes.'

It seemed to Grattan that they were talking about something else. Nothing was ever entirely as it seemed, he found himself thinking, and didn't know why he did.

'Different for yourself, I'd say, Mr Fitzmaurice.'

Grattan laughed. 'Oh, I knew what I was in for.'

They stood by the barbed-wire fence at the bottom of the garden, looking out into the shadows of pasture land beyond. Heifers were grazing there, but you could hardly see them now. Shadowy themselves, the two black-clad figures turned and walked back the way they'd come. It didn't seem likely, a sudden realization came to Grattan, that the priests had spoken in the way he'd thought, that the curate had been instructed in mercy and understanding. When you imagined, you were often wrong, and again he wondered why his visitor was here.

'It's a big old house,' Father Leahy said. 'It would always have been a rectory, would it?'

'Oh, it was built as a rectory all right. 1791.'

'It'll see a few years yet.'

'A lot of the clergy would prefer something smaller these days.'

'But not yourself?'

'You're used to a place.'

In front of the house again, twilight giving way to the dark now, they stood by Father Leahy's car, a silence gathering, the small talk of the conversation running out. Oisín ambled over the gravel and settled himself patiently on the front-door steps. Father Leahy said:

'I never knew a place as peaceful.'

'Any time you're near by come in again, Father.'

There was the flare of a match, then the glow of the priest's cigarette, tobacco pleasant on the evening air, mingling with the flowers.

'It wasn't easy, I dare say.' Father Leahy's face was lost in the dark now, only the glow of the cigarette's tip moving, his voice trailing off.

'Easy, Father?'

'I meant for yourself.'

It seemed to Grattan that it was possible to say that in the dark, when it hadn't been before, that truth could flourish in the dark, that in the dark communication was easier.

'Time was, a priest in Ireland wouldn't read the *Irish Times*. Father MacPartlan remarks on that. But we take it in now.'

'I thought maybe that picture –'

'There's more to it all than what that picture says.'

Something about the quiet tone of voice bewildered Grattan. And there were intimations beneath the tone that startled him. Father Leahy said:

'It's where we've ended.'

So softly that was spoken, Grattan hardly heard it, and then it was repeated, increasing his bewilderment. Why did it seem he was being told that the confidence the priests possessed was a surface that lingered beyond its day? Why, listening, did he receive that intimation? Why did it seem he was being told there was illusion, somewhere, in the solemn voices, hands raised in blessing, the holy water, the cross made in the air? At Ennismolach, long ago, there had been the traps and the side-cars and the dog-carts lined up along the Sunday verges, as the cars were lined up now outside the Church of the Holy Assumption. The same sense of nourishment there'd been, the safe foundation on a rock that could not shatter. Why did it seem he was being reminded of that past?

'But surely,' he began to say, and changed his mind, leaving the two words uselessly on their own. He often read in the paper these days that in the towns Mass was not as well attended as it had been even a few years ago. In the towns marriage was not always bothered with, confession and absolution passed by. A different culture, they called it, in which restraint and prayer were not the way, as once they had been. Crime spread in the different culture, they said, and drugs taken by children, and old women raped, and murder. A plague it was, and it would reach the country too, was reaching it already. The jolly Norbertine man of God grinned from the newspaper photograph in village shops and farmhouse kitchens, on cottage dressers, propped up against milk jugs at mealtimes, and he grinned again on television screens. Would he say that all he ever did was to reach out and gather in his due, that God had made him so? In the different culture Christ's imitation offered too little.

'I often think of those monks on the islands,' Father Leahy said. 'Any acre they'd spot out on the sea they would row off to to see could they start a community there.'

'They would.'

'Cowled against the wind. Or cowled against what's left behind. Afraid, Father MacPartlan says. When Father Mac-Partlan comes in to breakfast you can see the rims of his eyes red.'

An image of the older priest was vivid for a moment in Grattan's recall, his mourning black, the collar cutting into pink flesh, hair that had thinned and gone grey over the years of their acquaintanceship. That this man wept in the night was barely credible.

'I never left Ireland,' Father Leahy said. 'I have never been outside it.'

'Nor I.' The silence after that was part of the dark, easily there, not awkward. And Grattan said, 'I love Ireland.'

They loved it in different ways: unspoken in the dark, that was another intimation. For Grattan there was history's tale, regrets and sorrows and distress, the voices of unconquered men, the spirit of women as proud as empresses. For Grattan there were the rivers he knew, the mountains he had never climbed, wild fuchsia by a seashore and the swallows that came back, turf smoke on the air of little towns, the quiet in long glens. The sound, the look, the shape of Ireland, and Ireland's rain and Ireland's sunshine, and Ireland's living and Ireland's dead: all that.

On Sundays, when Mass was said and had been said again, Father Leahy stood in a crowd watching the men of Kildare and Kerry, of Offaly and Meath, yelling out encouragement, deploring some lack of skill. And afterwards he took his pint as any man might, talking the game through. For Father Leahy there was the memory of the cars going by, his bare feet on the cobbles of the yard, the sacrifice he had made, and his faithful coming to him, the cross emblazoned on a holy robe. Good Catholic Ireland, a golden age.

'Anywhere you'd be,' Grattan said, 'there's always change. Like day becoming night.'

'I know. Sure, I know of course.'

Father Leahy's cigarette dropped on to the ground. There was the sound of his shoe crunching away the spark left in the butt, then his footsteps began on the gravel. A light came on when he opened the car door.

'You're not left bereft, you know,' Grattan said.

'Father MacPartlan looked over the table tonight after he'd put sugar in his tea. What he said to me was you'd given Con Tonan his life back. Even though Con Tonan wasn't one of your own.'

'Ah, no, no, I didn't do that.'

'D'you know the way it sometimes is, you want to tell a person a thing?'

The curate's hand was held out in the little pool of light, and there was the same friendliness in the clasp before he started the car's engine.

'Father Leahy called in last night,' Grattan heard himself reporting to Mrs Bradshaw. 'The first time a priest ever came to the rectory that I remember.' And Mrs Bradshaw, astonished, would think about it all morning while she worked, and would probably say before she left that the curate calling in was an expression of the ecumenical spirit they were all on about these days. Something like that.

For a few more minutes Grattan remained outside, a trace of tobacco smoke still in the garden, the distant hum of the curate's car not quite gone. The future was frightening for Father Leahy, as it had been for the monks who rowed away from Ireland once, out on to their rocks; as it had been for his father on his deathbed. But the monks and his father had escaped, mercy granted them. The golden age of the bishops was vanishing in a drama that was as violent as the burning of the houses and the fleeing of the families, and old priests like Father MacPartlan were made melancholy by their loss and passed their melancholy on.

'Come on, Oisín,' Grattan called, for his dog had wandered in the garden. 'Come on now.'

He had paid Con Tonan what he could; he'd been glad of his company. He had never thought of Con Tonan in his garden as a task he'd been given, as a single tendril of the vine to make his own. But the priest had come this evening to say it had been so, and by saying it had found a solace for himself. Small gestures mattered now, and statements in the dark were a way to keep the faith, as the monks had kept it in an Ireland that was different too.

Good News

'Hi,' the bald man with the earrings said. 'I'm Roland.'

He looked at Bea from behind small, round spectacles. She watched his gaze passing slowly over her features, over her shoulders and her chest, her hands on the table between them. Bea was nine, with dark hair that was long, and brown eyes with a dreamy look that was sometimes mistaken for sadness.

'You're going to show us, Leah?' the man with earrings said, and the girl who stood beside him, in a navy-blue jumper and jeans, ran a finger down a list on her clipboard and told him the name was Bea.

'Take your time, Leah,' the man said.

Bea had practised, the curtains drawn so that it was dark, Iris suddenly switching on the table lamp. Waking up on the sofa, wondering where she was, was what was marked on the script as the bit they would ask her to do.

She crossed to where two chairs were drawn close together to represent the sofa. She lay down on them and waited for the girl with the clipboard to say she'd switched the light on, as she'd said she would. Bea's hands went up then, shielding her eyes, not making too much of the gesture, not milking it, as Iris had explained you never should, subtlety being everything.

'Quite nice,' the man with the earrings said.

*

Iris was Bea's mother. Iris Stebbing she'd been born, but she'd turned that into Iris Orlando for professional purposes, and Iris Adams she'd become when she married Dickie. It was several years since she had gone for a part herself – 'woman in massage parlour' – which they'd said at the last minute she wasn't quite right for. Occasionally she still rang up about a forthcoming production she'd read about in *The Stage* and they always promised to bear her in mind. But they never rang back.

Bea was different, with everything ahead of her. And Bea had talent, Iris was certain of that. She could see her one day as Ophelia, or the young just-married in *Outward Bound*, which she had played herself, or Rachel-Elizabeth in *Bring on the Night*. Iris had taught Bea all she knew.

Another child came in to wait, with a stout young woman who was presumably a mother too, unhealthy-looking, Iris considered. The child was timid, which of course was what they wanted, but rabbity in appearance, which Iris doubted they'd want, not for a minute. Bea was quiet, always had been, but she didn't look half dead. More to the point, she didn't have teeth like that.

'Hi,' the mother said.

Iris wrinkled her lips a bit, the smile she gave to strangers.

There would be others, of course. Every fifteen minutes, they'd keep coming all morning. She knew the drill.

Iris was not a young mother herself. She hadn't wanted to have children, but when she reached forty she had suddenly felt panicky, which of course – she readily admitted – was her all over. She had a part in the hospital serial then, but she'd begun to think she'd never have another one. The last year in Wanstead it was. Dickie was still on the road, office stationery.

Another mother and another child came in, the mother even younger than the fat one, the child brazen-faced, not right at all. They liked to be early, half an hour at least, and this time there was no greeting, nothing said, no smiles. Competitiveness had taken over; Iris could feel it in herself, a mounting dislike of those she shared the small waiting-room with.

'There we are,' the girl in the navy-blue jumper and jeans said, bringing Bea back. 'You like to come in now?' she invited the rabbity child, and shook her head when the mother attempted to accompany her. 'We'll call you this evening,' she said to Iris, 'if Bea has been successful. After five it'll be. All right, after five?'

Iris said it would be, handing Bea her coat. They didn't say 'Don't ring us' any more, a joke it had become. But she remembered when it wasn't.

A mother and child were on the way in as they left and Iris stared quickly at the child: lumpy, you couldn't call her anything else, and thin hair with a grey tinge.

'Let's have a coffee,' Iris said on the street.

*

Bea was thinking about Dickie. When Iris had come off the phone and said there'd be an audition she had thought about him; and ever since, while they were practising and going through the script, he'd kept coming into her mind. It was two years since the quarrel about the shirts, when Iris said she'd had enough and Dickie went off, the summer before last, a Monday.

'They say they liked you?' Iris asked in the café. 'They say anything?'

Bea shook her head, then pushed back her hair where it had fallen over her forehead. John's the café was called, all done out in green, which Bea liked because it was her favourite colour. They sat at a counter that ran along the windows and a girl brought them cappuccinos.

'They only said about the waking up,' Bea said.

When she'd told Dickie about the audition he'd stopped suddenly as they were walking across the dusty grass in the Wild Park. She'd told him then because Iris said she should, the Sunday after it was all fixed up. He'd stood perfectly still, looking into the trees in the distance, then he turned and looked down at her. That was marvellous, he said.

'They wanted you to do it with the movements?' Iris asked. 'Like I showed you?'

Bea shook her head. They didn't want movements, she said. The man called her Leah, she said.

'Leah? My God, he thought you were one of the others! My God!'

'He didn't understand "Bea".'

She'd known what was passing through Dickie's thoughts

when he heard the news in the Wild Park. She'd known because of the other times there'd been good news – when Iris won fifteen pounds in the milkman's draw, when Dickie was in work again one time, when Iris's aunt died and there was the will. Dickie had been invited in the Sunday after the milkman's draw and there'd been a bottle of wine. 'He still holding on to that job?' Iris would ask, but he hadn't, not for long; and the will had brought only the fish cutlery. But even so, good news when it came always brightened things up where Dickie and Iris were concerned, and one of these days it wouldn't just go away again. Quite often Bea felt sure of that.

'You told that man, though? You said about the name?'

'The girl knew.'

'You said it to her? You're sure?'

'She had it written down.'

It was July, warm and airless, no sign of the sun. It pleased Bea that all this had occurred when the summer holidays were about to start and no one in her class would have to know she was in an audition for a TV thing. 'Of course you'll have to say,' Iris had said, 'if you get the part. On account they'll see you when it comes on.'

Bea thought she probably wouldn't. It could even be they wouldn't recognize her, which was what she'd like. She didn't know why she wanted that, at the same time wanting so much to get the part because of Dickie. 'So what kind of a story is it?' Dickie had asked in the Wild Park and she said a woman was murdered in it.

'Practise a bit?' Iris said when they were back in the flat, after they'd had clam chowder and salad.

Bea didn't want to, now that the audition was over, but Iris said it would pass the time. So they practised for an hour and then sat by the open window, listening to the sound of the traffic coming from Chalmers Street, watching the people going by, the afternoon turned sunny at last. 'Don't be disappointed,' Iris kept saying, and when the telephone rang at a quarter to six she said it could be anyone. It could be Dickie about tomorrow, or the telephone people, who often rang at this time on a Saturday to explain some scheme or other, offering free calls if you did what they wanted you to do.

But it was the girl in the navy-blue jumper to say that Bea had got the part.

*

The rehearsals took place in an army drill-hall. Iris had to be there too, and at the studios where the set was, and on location. She had arranged to take her holiday specially; and it worried Bea that she intended to call in sick when the holiday time ran out. 'I *know* this place!' she cried, excitedly looking round the drill-hall when they walked into it the first morning.

'A while ago now,' Bea heard her telling the woman who'd said she was playing the bag-lady. She'd had great ambitions, Iris said, but then the marriage and all that had been a setback. He'd been out of work for six years as near's no matter, and then again later of course. A regular thing it became and she'd had to take what was going in a typing pool. Ruinous that was, as she'd known it would be, as anyone in the profession could guess.

'The kiddie'll make it up to you,' the bag-lady predicted. 'Definitely,' she added, as if making up herself for not sounding interested enough.

'When the call came I couldn't believe it. "Ring Dickie," I said. Well, it's only fair, no matter what the past.'

'A father'd want to know. Any father would.'

'She's had to have her hair cut off.'

Bea listened to these exchanges because there was nothing else to do. When she'd rung Dickie to tell him he'd said immediately that he was over the moon and she knew he was. 'You say well done to Iris for me,' he'd said, and immediately she had imagined him coming back to the flat, as sometimes she did, arriving with his two old suitcases. 'Well, what d'you know!' he'd kept saying on the phone. 'Well, I never!'

He liked Bea to call him Dickie because she called Iris Iris; he liked the warmth of it, he said. 'Remember the time we stayed in the hotel?' he often reminded her, having once taken her to Brighton for a night. 'Remember the day we saw the accident, the bus going too fast? Remember the first time in the Wild Park?'

He was big and awkward, given to knocking things over. He had another child, dark-skinned, who didn't live with him either. 'You tell her good old Iris,' he said on the phone, giving credit where it was due because he knew Iris had been trying for this for years. 'You won't forget now, old girl?'

Any excuse, he'd be back. When he said he was over the moon it was because this was the kind of chance that could change everything. Bea saw him once a fortnight, a week on

Sunday the next time was and he'd said he couldn't wait.

'Hi, Bea,' the man called Roland said, getting her name right when they were all sitting down at the drill-hall's long trestle-table. The girl in the navy-blue jumper had a walkie-talkie attached to her clipboard, and a badge with *Andi* on it. A boy with fuzzy hair was handing round biscuits, and coffee in paper cups. 'Best coffee in London,' he kept saying and sometimes someone laughed.

Bea watched while the scripts were leafed through, some of them being marked with a ballpoint. She turned the pages of hers, finding page fourteen, which was where she came into it, even though in the whole script she didn't actually speak. 'Mr Hance,' the man who came to sit in the chair next to hers introduced himself as, giving the name of the character he played. He was thin and lank, with milky eyes beneath a squashed forehead, his grey suit spotted a bit, his tie a tight knot in an uncomfortable-looking collar. 'You've dressed the part,' Bea had heard Andi saying to him.

'From the top,' Roland called out, and the drill-hall went silent. Then the voices began.

It was the old woman with the dyed red hair who was murdered. In the drill-hall her elderliness was disguised with bright crimson lipstick and the henna in her hair. Mr Hance put the poison in the yoghurt carton that was left with her milk on Wednesdays and Fridays. Iris had explained all that, but Bea understood it better when she heard the voices in the drill-hall.

Not that she understood everything. In the script it said that Mr Hance played marbles with her, which was a game no one Bea knew played or had an interest in. 'That's a very lonely man,' Iris had said, but it seemed peculiar to Bea that a lonely person wouldn't go to the pub or some billiard hall instead of playing marbles with a child in a car park. In the script she was meant to be lonely herself; 'Little Miss Latchkey' Mr Hance called her because there was never anyone at home to let her in. In the script it said the old woman had tidy white hair, and a walking-stick because she couldn't manage without one.

Iris was happy from the moment they entered the drill-hall: Bea could tell. She remembered it all so well, Bea heard her telling the bag-lady and later Ann-Marie, the newsagent's daughter. The gossip of the profession, the knitting while you waited for your cue, the puffing at a cigarette you didn't want when something wasn't going right: Iris was back where she belonged, among the friends she might have had.

In the late afternoon there was the funeral scene: the clergyman's words ringing out, the mourners standing round a chalked rectangle on the floor, the old woman who was dead completing the *Daily Telegraph* crossword. When the burial was over the boy with the fuzzy hair was given the task of showing Bea and Mr Hance how to play marbles.

'All right then, Bea?' Andi asked a few times, and Bea said she was. It was probably not being tall, she thought, that gave Andi the heavy look she had heard her complaining about earlier. She was on a slimming course, she'd said, but it didn't seem to be doing any good. Bea liked her best of all the people in the drill-hall.

'From the top one more time,' Roland called out when

Bea thought the rehearsing must surely be over, and they went through the whole script again. She hadn't shared her mother's pleasure in the day. She hadn't known what to expect, any more than she'd known what to expect at the audition. When the script had come in Iris said that the only disappointment was that Bea didn't ever get to speak. She had remarked as much to Ann-Marie while the funeral scene was going on, mouthing it so as not to interrupt. And Ann-Marie, who was pussy-faced, Bea thought, but very pretty, waited until the funeral scene was over to say that Bea's part was all the more telling for being silent. Bea had been glad she didn't have to say anything, but she wondered now if it might perhaps be less boring if she had to say just a little.

*

'How's it going, Beasie?'

Dickie's brown jacket needed a stitch at the pocket that was nearer to her, on a level with her eyes when she looked. It needed more of a stitch than it had two Sundays ago, which was the last time she'd seen it. He was incapable of attending to his clothes, Iris said.

'OK,' Bea said. Three weeks had passed since the first day in the drill-hall and the drill-hall had long ago been left behind. They'd moved into the set at the studios, and there'd been days of filming on location.

'You tell Iris what I said that time, Beasie? You say I said well done?'

She nodded, cold on the street where they were walking

even though it was August. She dug her hands into the pockets of the coat Iris had said to take in case it rained. The Sunday before last she'd said she'd told Iris.

'I told her,' she said again.

He hadn't seen Iris today. He hadn't seen her the last Sunday either. He'd rung the bell and Bea had called down on the intercom and he'd waited for her, the same both times.

'All these years,' he said on the street, '*The Stage*'s been her Bible.'

'Yes.'

And in the end it was *The Stage* that came up trumps. Dickie went on talking about that, and Bea imagined her mother inviting him in. One Sunday or another, she said to herself, sooner or later. 'We must tell Dickie,' Iris had kept saying during the three weeks that had passed – about Ann-Marie being half asleep in the early morning and letting the piles of newspapers she'd just opened fall off the counter, and how she put back the different sections any old how; about Mr Hance and the marbles; about the caged canary still singing when the old woman lay dead.

'Doesn't worry you, any of that stuff?' Dickie had said in the Wild Park when she'd shown him in the script where the murder was. 'If it worries you, you say, old girl.'

She never would. She didn't tell Iris when she dreamed about the dog on the garbage tip, the microbes you could see moving through its entrails in the film sequence. In the viewing-room, with the red light showing outside, she had sat with the others, not knowing what it was the police were looking for on the tip, watching while the camera crept slowly over the entrails of the dog. She didn't know why the old woman kept rapping with her stick on the window, why she kept sitting there and then rapping again. 'She's a peeper,' was all Mr Hance said in the script, and in the long waits when Bea wasn't involved the confusion made the boredom worse.

'What's that Hance like?' Dickie asked.

'All right.' Bea didn't say she didn't like him. She said it was a joke that he was always called Mr Hance. Extra pages had gone into his script, yellow pages at first, the second batch pink. She hadn't been given any herself, but she could see the colours showing at the edges when he sat beside her in the coach, on the way to the studios or the locations. He always sat beside her. Getting to know her, Iris said.

'Iris think he's good?' Dickie asked.

'Oh, yes.'

They all did. He took pains, they said; he found his way. 'She wasn't very nice, you know,' he said about the old woman, talking about her in the room where Bea had to wake up on the sofa. He often didn't look at you when he spoke and because of his whispery voice you sometimes couldn't hear. Bea didn't know why Mr Hance made her nervous, why he had even on the first day, why most of all he did when he sat beside her in the coach, one of his fingers tracing over and over again the outline of the little label that was sewn into the edge of his plain brown scarf. On every journey his milky eyes turned away from the coach window before the journey ended and his fingers became still. He gazed at her, saying nothing, and at first she thought he was practising the part. She'd seen them doing that, trying something out, hearing one another's lines, but in the coach it didn't seem like practising. The room with the sofa in it was in his house, where he took her after the old woman was dead, the sofa all sagging and old, two empty milk bottles on the window-sill, cat litter on the floor beneath it. They kept having to do the scene in which she woke up, getting it right.

'We take in a film today?' Dickie suggested. '*Meet Me in St Louis*'s come back.' In the cinema, listening to the songs, Bea tried not to think about being bored again tomorrow or Mr Hance making her nervous in the coach. She tried not to see the moisture on his squashed forehead when he knelt down by the sofa and asked her to forgive him. She tried not to hear him saying something she couldn't hear in the coach, or not saying anything when he gazed at her.

'Wasn't that grand!' Dickie said when Judy Garland sang for the last time and *The End* went up on the screen. 'I've got some hot-cross buns,' he said when they were on the street, although it wasn't Easter, the wrong time of year by ages. In his bedsitting-room they toasted the hot-cross buns because they were a bit on the stale side. They squatted on the floor, each of them with a fork, poking their buns at the bar of the electric fire.

It was warm in the bedsitting-room, Dickie's overcoat hanging from the hook on the back of the door, his bed under the sloping windows, a curtain drawn over so you wouldn't know the sink was there. He had little sachets of jam, blackcurrant and strawberry, and he offered her a choice.

'There's Swiss roll,' he said, and he laughed. What was left of one, he meant. He'd kept it for her. 'Iris busy this evening?' he asked when they had finished everything. 'Going out, is she?'

Bea shook her head, but when they got to the flat Iris didn't ask him in. Iris wasn't sure yet, Bea said to herself, and later on, when she was in bed, she went over the signs there'd been – Iris saying they must tell Dickie about the audition and then about Ann-Marie and the newspapers, and the canary singing. But when Bea fell asleep it wasn't Dickie being back that came into her dreams. In the room with the milk bottles on the window-sill Mr Hance was showing her the label on his scarf and she kept saying she must go now. She kept trying to get up from the sofa but she couldn't.

*

'It's like you pity Mr Hance,' Roland said, turning a chair round so that he was facing Bea in the viewing-room. He dangled a leg over one of the chair's arms, which was his favourite way of sitting. His earrings were crucifixes, Bea noticed, which she hadn't before. 'The piece is about stuff like that, chick.'

Yesterday on the screen Mr Hance had walked away from the funeral and then walked on, through the streets by the river and the gasometers. In a startling way his features had suddenly filled the screen, tears glistening on his lean cheeks.

'We're into compassion here,' Roland said.

Bea tried to blank out Mr Hance's weeping face, which she could still see even though the screen was empty now.

The tears ran down to the corners of his mouth, droplets becoming snagged there or slipping on, into the crevices of his chin.

'Like some poor wounded bird,' Roland said. 'Some little sparrow with a smashed-up wing. And you'd be sorry for it because maybe the other sparrows would be quicker and take the crumbs. You're with us here, Bea?'

Her mother looked sharply at her, which quite reminded her of a sparrow's beady gaze. Bea knew Iris was being sharp because she didn't want her to say she didn't like feathers, that they never put crumbs out because of that. The time in Trafalgar Square the pigeons were frightening the way they rushed by you, their wings crashing into your face. 'Never again,' Dickie had promised. 'You give your nuts to that little boy there.' But she hadn't wanted even to do that. She didn't want to have the nuts in her hand for a minute longer.

'Try for it, shall we?' Roland said. 'The pity thing?'

Bea began to nod. 'Why'd he have to murder her?' she asked, because she had always wondered that.

'Because the friendship's going to be taken from him.' Roland swung his leg off the arm of the chair. 'Because the old lady's got the wrong end of the stick. OK, chick?'

Bea said it was, because there didn't seem much point in saying anything else. She had asked Iris where the dog's carcass on the tip came into it, if the dog had been the old woman's or what, and Iris said they would understand that when the film was put together. They would understand where Ann-Marie arranging the newspapers came into it, and the bag-lady looking in the lamp-post bins for any food that was thrown away, and the workmen repairing a pavement, and the man in a maroon-coloured car. The trouble was, Iris said, that the scenes hadn't been shot in the right order, which naturally made it difficult. The yoghurt the poison had been put in was banana and guava, and Bea said to herself that never in her whole life would she eat banana and guava yoghurt again. One morning on the coach Mr Hance asked her what colour her school uniform was and she felt panicky when he did although she didn't know why, just a simple question it was. She wanted to get up, to find some place else to sit, but moving about the coach would draw attention to her and she didn't want that. 'It's all just pretend,' Mr Hance said another day. 'Only pretend, Bea.' It seemed strange to say that, to say what she already knew, and she wondered if she'd misheard because of Mr Hance's quiet voice.

Once when the coach drew up and they all got out, when Bea was walking with Iris to the location, she wanted so much to say she was frightened of Mr Hance that she almost did. She began to, but Iris luckily wasn't listening. Bea realized at once that it was lucky. Everything would have been ruined.

*

'Let's go for it this time, chick,' Roland said on the last day, going for the final take. Bea could hear the soft whirring of the camera when the fuzzy-haired boy had given the take number and clapped the clapperboard. They had practised the scene before the coffee break and again after it, when Roland had repeated all he'd said about pity.

Bea couldn't do it in the take any more than she'd been able to when they'd practised. 'Cut!' the fuzzy-haired boy had to keep exclaiming, and Roland came on to the set and talked to Bea again, and Iris came on because he asked her to. 'Sorry,' Bea kept saying.

The make-up girls came on in the end. They gave her artificial tears, and the cameraman said that was better by a long chalk. The lighting man changed the lighting, softening it considerably.

'We'll go for it this time,' Roland said, and the fuzzy-haired boy held up the clapperboard and called out another number. 'One more time,' Roland said when Bea had lost count of the takes.

They ran fifteen minutes into the lunch break before they dispersed and made their way to the mobile canteen. Over a chicken salad with chips, Iris recalled for the bag-lady and the police inspector the part she'd had – a child herself then – in an episode of *Z Cars*, 1962 it was. Bea had heard this a few times before and, since she didn't like the bean-and-sausage bake she'd helped herself to, she looked around for somewhere to get rid of it without anyone, especially Iris, noticing. Iris always said to eat well at the mobile canteen so that there wouldn't have to be much cooking when they got back to the flat. But there was no convenient vase or fire bucket into which to tip the load on Bea's cardboard plate. Outside, where the cars were parked, she found the dustbins.

After that she didn't want to go back to where the mobile canteen was set up because they'd see she wasn't eating anything and press a lot of stuff she didn't want on her. She walked about the empty set, which she had never had to herself before. She wandered from room to room, thinking it was a pity that soon it would all be dismantled when the homeless who slept in doorways could do with it, even if only for a night.

'Hullo,' a voice said just before Bea heard Mr Hance's footstep, and she knew he had come looking for her.

*

That evening Dickie came to the party. 'You ask your father,' Iris had said. 'Only fair.' Dickie had said yes at once.

'Under time, under budget!' Roland announced in his speech of gratitude to the cast, and everyone clapped.

They were all there on the set – the bag-lady, Ann-Marie, the police inspector, the old woman, the man in the maroon car, the workmen who'd been repairing a pavement, the policemen who'd searched the tip, Mr Hance.

They made a fuss of Mr Hance. It was his piece, they said, his show. 'I've heard a lot about you,' Dickie said to him, and Bea thought he hadn't really, but Dickie was good at being polite. The tear by his jacket pocket hadn't been repaired. Bea had seen Iris noticing it when Dickie came over to say hullo.

'So what's next on the agenda?' the police inspector asked Bea. 'Another part lined up, have we?'

'Spoilt for choice,' Iris said, but Bea wondered about that, and Dickie said what's this then? A certain little lady on her way was what, the police inspector said.

All the technicians and production people were at the

party – the sound man, the cameraman and the assistant cameraman, the set designer, the make-up girls, the costume girls, the continuity girl. They drank wine, red or white, and there was Coca Cola or orange juice to go with the plates of cold food. Dickie asked who the big woman with the glasses on a chain was and Iris said the producer. 'Remember that producer on *Emergency Ward 10?*' Dickie said.

'Oh, my God, don't!'

Music began. Bea showed Dickie about the set: Mr Hance's room with the cat litter still there, the stairs, the hall with the antlers, the living-room of the other house, where the old woman rapped the window with her walking-stick. 'Marvellous,' Dickie kept saying. One part of the set had been dismantled already and Iris came along to explain all that.

Andi and the boy with fuzzy hair brought round the wine and the food. Roland knocked on the floor with the old woman's walking-stick: early as it was, he said, he had to be going. They'd been great, he complimented everyone. Pure electricity this production was, the Good Housekeeping Seal.

There was laughter, and more applause. Roland waved good-bye with the walking-stick, then handed it to Andi. After he'd gone someone turned the music up.

When no one was looking, Bea opened the sandwich she had taken. There seemed to be scrambled egg in it so she dropped it into an empty cardboard box beside where she was standing. She was alone there, obscured by the pot plants that had been gathered together on a table, ready to go back to *Flowers Etc*, which was what was scrawled on a piece of paper tied around one of them. She could see Dickie and Iris and Mr Hance, the sound man seeming to be telling them a story. When he came to the end of it they laughed, Iris particularly, throwing back her head in a way she had. Still pouring wine, the boy with the fuzzy hair looked to where the laughter had come from and laughed himself, then moved over to fill their glasses up.

Peeping through the fleshy green leaves, Bea watched Mr Hance earnestly talking now, Dickie's head bent to listen. A moment ago Iris had held on to Dickie's arm, just for a second when one of her high heels let her down. She had reached out and clutched at him and he had smiled at her and she had smiled herself. Where they were standing was quite near where Bea had been when Mr Hance had said hullo that afternoon.

Across the set the old woman was sitting on her own, a cigarette alight, her wine glass half full. With her painted features and bright dyed hair she didn't at all look like the old woman by the window, but in spite of that she still was, and suddenly Bea wanted to go over to her and say she'd been right. She wanted her to know. She wanted just one person to know.

'Hi, Bea,' Andi said. 'That your dad, then?'

'Yes.'

'He looks nice. Nice way he has.'

'Yes.'

'Not in the profession, though? Not like your mum?' Andi reached out to feel one of the leaves, softly caressing it between forefinger and thumb. 'He could get a walk-on, your dad. You never know.'

Andi seemed forlorn without her clipboard and mobile telephone, wearing the same blue jumper she'd worn for all six weeks of the production. She wasn't drinking wine; she wasn't eating anything, but that would be because of her slimming.

'You going for it, Bea? You reckon?' She'd gone for it herself only it hadn't worked out. She wasn't right for the acting side of the business, although it was what she'd wanted at first. 'Different for you,' Andi said.

'Yes.'

It would be better to tell Andi. It would be easier to say it had to be a secret, that all she wanted was one person to know. It seemed mean not to tell Andi when she'd come over specially to be friendly.

'Maybe our paths'll cross again,' Andi said. 'Anyway I hope they do.'

'Yes.'

'You did fine.'

Bea shook her head. Through the foliage she saw Mr Hance's hand held out, to her mother and then to Dickie. They smiled at him, and then he made his way through the other people at the party, stepping over the electrical cables that stretched from one room of the set to another. Occasionally he stopped to shake hands or to be embraced. The old woman laughed up at him, sharing some joke.

'I must make my farewells.' Andi kissed Bea and said again she hoped their paths would cross some time.

'So do I.' Bea tried to tell Andi then. But if Andi knew it might show in her face even if she didn't want it to. It mightn't be easy for her not to let it, and when someone asked her what the matter was it could slip out when she wasn't thinking.

'Cheers,' Andi said.

The bag-lady was going also. In the corner where the cameras still were, outside the set itself, Ann-Marie was dancing with one of the policemen. Dickie was holding up Iris's see-through plastic mackintosh, waiting for Iris to step into it. 'See you on the ice,' the fuzzy-haired boy called after Mr Hance, and Mr Hance waved back at him before he walked out of the brightness that was the party.

*

On the train Iris told Dickie who everyone was, which part each had played, who was who among the technicians. Dickie asked questions to keep her going.

It was the first time Bea had made the journey in from the studios by train. There had always been the coach before, to the studios and back, to whatever the location was. The train was nicer, the houses that backed on to the railway line lit up, here and there people still in their gardens even though it was dark. Sometimes the train stopped at a suburban station, the passengers who alighted seeming weary as they made their way along the platform. 'I must say, I enjoyed that,' Dickie said.

They got the last bus to Chalmers Street and walked, all three of them, to the flat. 'Come in, Dickie?' Iris invited.

She'd got in the cereal he liked and it was there on the kitchen table, ready for breakfast. Bea saw him noticing it.

'Good night, old girl,' he said, and Bea kissed him, and

kissed Iris too, for Iris had said she was too tired to come in to say good-night.

Bea washed, and folded her clothes, and brushed her teeth. She turned the light out, wondering in what way her dreams would be different now, reminding herself that she mustn't cry out in case, being sleepy, she ruined everything.

The Mourning

In the town, on the grey estate on the Dunmanway road,
they lived in a corner house. They always had. Mrs Brogan
had borne and brought up six children there. Brogan, a
council labourer, still grew vegetables and a few marigolds
in its small back garden. Only Liam Pat was still at home with
them, at twenty-three the youngest in the family, working for
O'Dwyer the builder. His mother – his father, too, though
in a different way – was upset when Liam Pat said he was
thinking of moving further afield. 'Cork?' his mother asked.
But it was England Liam Pat had in mind.

Dessie Coglan said he could get him fixed. He'd go himself,
Dessie Coglan said, if he didn't have the wife and another
kid expected. No way Rosita would stir, no way she'd move
five yards from the estate, with her mother two doors down.
'You'll fall on your feet there all right,' Dessie Coglan confi-
dently predicted. 'No way you won't.'

Liam Pat didn't have wild ambitions; but he wanted to
make what he could of himself. At the Christian Brothers'
he'd been the tidiest in the class. He'd been attentive, even
though he often didn't understand. Father Mooney used to
compliment him on the suit he always put on for Mass,
handed down through the family, and the tie he always wore

on Sundays. 'The respect, Liam Pat,' Father Mooney would say. 'It's heartening for your old priest to see the respect, to see you'd give the boots a brush.' Shoes, in fact, were what Liam Pat wore to Sunday Mass, black and patched, handed down also. Although they didn't keep out the wet, that didn't deter him from wearing them in the rain, stuffing them with newspaper when he was home again. 'Ah, sure, you'll pick it up,' O'Dwyer said when Liam Pat asked him if he could learn a trade. He'd pick up the whole lot – plumbing, bricklaying, carpentry, house-painting. He'd have them all at his finger-tips; if he settled for one of them, he wouldn't get half the distance. Privately, O'Dwyer's opinion was that Liam Pat didn't have enough upstairs to master any trade and when it came down to it what was wrong with operating the mixer? 'Keep the big mixer turning and keep Liam Pat Brogan behind it,' was one of O'Dwyer's good-humoured catch-phrases on the sites where his men built houses for him. 'Typical O'Dwyer,' Dessie Coglan scornfully pronounced. Stay with O'Dwyer and Liam Pat would be shovelling wet cement for the balance of his days.

Dessie was on the estate also. He had married into it, getting a house when the second child was born. Dessie had had big ideas at the Brothers'; with a drink or two in him he had them still. There was his talk of 'the lads' and of 'connections' with the extreme republican movement, his promotion of himself as a fixer. By trade he was a plasterer.

'Give that man a phone as soon as you're there,' he instructed Liam Pat, and Liam Pat wrote the number down. He had always admired Dessie, the easy way he had with

Rosita Drudy before he married her, the way he seemed to know how a hurling match would go even though he had never handled a hurley stick himself, the way he could talk through the cigarette he was smoking, his voice becoming so low you couldn't hear what he was saying, his eyes narrowed to lend weight to the confidential nature of what he passed on. A few people said Dessie Coglan was all mouth, but Liam Pat disagreed.

It's not bad at all, Liam Pat wrote on a postcard when he'd been in London a week. *There's a lad from Lismore and another from Westmeath.* Under a foreman called Huxter he was operating a cement-mixer and filling in foundations. He got lonely was what he didn't add to his message. *The wage is twice what O'Dwyer gave,* he squeezed in instead at the bottom of the card, which had a picture of a guardsman in a sentry-box on it.

Mrs Brogan put it on the mantelpiece. She felt lonely herself, as she'd known she would, the baby of the family gone. Brogan went out to the garden, trying not to think of the kind of place London was. Liam Pat was headstrong, like his mother, Mr Brogan considered. Good-natured but headstrong, the same red hair on the pair of them till her own had gone grey on her. He had asked Father Mooney to have a word with Liam Pat, but the damn bit of good it had done.

After that, every four weeks or so, Liam Pat telephoned on a Saturday evening. They always hoped they'd hear that he was about to return, but all he talked about was a job finished or a new job begun, how he waited every morning to be picked up by the van, to be driven halfway across

London from the area where he had a room. The man who was known to Dessie Coglan had got him the work, as Dessie Coglan said he would. 'A Mr Huxter's on the lookout for young fellows,' the man, called Feeny, had said when Liam Pat phoned him as soon as he arrived in London. In his Saturday conversations – on each occasion with his mother first and then, more briefly, with his father – Liam Pat didn't reveal that when he'd asked Huxter about learning a trade the foreman had said take what was on offer or leave it, a general labourer was what was needed. Liam Pat didn't report, either, that from the first morning in the gang Huxter had taken against him, without a reason that Liam Pat could see. It was Huxter's way to pick on someone, they said in the gang.

They didn't wonder why, nor did Liam Pat. They didn't know that a victim was a necessary compensation for the shortages in Huxter's life – his wife's regular refusal to grant him what he considered to be his bedroom rights, the failure of a horse or greyhound; compensation, too, for surveyors' sarcasm and the pernicketiness of fancy-booted architects. A big, black-moustached man, Huxter worked as hard as any of the men under him, stripping himself to his vest, a brass buckle on the belt that held his trousers up. 'What kind of a name's that?' he said when Liam Pat told him, and called him Mick instead. There was something about Liam Pat's freckled features that grated on Huxter, and although he was well used to Irish accents he convinced himself that he couldn't understand this one. 'Oh, very Irish,' Huxter would say even when Liam Pat did something sensible, such as putting planks down in the mud to wheel the barrows on.

When Liam Pat had been working with Huxter for six weeks the man called Feeny got in touch again, on the phone one Sunday. 'How're you doing?' Feeny enquired. 'Are you settled, boy?'

Liam Pat said he was, and a few days later, when he was with the two other Irish boys from the gang, standing up at the bar in a public house called the Spurs and Horse, Feeny arrived in person. 'How're you doing?' Feeny said, introducing himself. He was a wizened-featured man with black hair in a widow's peak. He had a clerical look about him but he wasn't a priest, as he soon made clear. He worked in a glass factory, he said.

He shook hands with all three of them, with Rafferty and Noonan as warmly as with Liam Pat. He bought them drinks, refusing to let them pay for his, saying he couldn't allow young fellows. A bit of companionship was all he was after, he said. 'Doesn't it keep the poor exile going?'

There was general agreement with this sentiment. There were some who came over, Feeny said, who stayed no longer than a few days. 'Missing the mam,' he said, his thin lips drawn briefly back to allow a laugh that Rafferty remarked afterwards reminded him of the bark of a dog. 'A young fellow one time didn't step out of the train,' Feeny said.

After that, Feeny often looked in at the Spurs and Horse. In subsequent conversations, asking questions and showing an interest, he learnt that Huxter was picking on Liam Pat. He didn't know Huxter personally, he said, but both Rafferty and Noonan assured him that Liam Pat had cause for more complaint than he admitted to, that when Huxter got going he was no bloody joke. Feeny sympathized, tightening his mouth in a way he had, wagging his head in disgust. It was perhaps because of what he heard, Rafferty and Noonan deduced, that Feeny made a particular friend of Liam Pat, more than he did of either of them, which was fair enough in the circumstances.

Feeny took Liam Pat to greyhound tracks; he found him a better place to live; he lent him money when Liam Pat was short once, and didn't press for repayment. As further weeks went by, everything would have been all right as far as Liam Pat was concerned if it hadn't been for Huxter. 'Ah, no, I'm grand,' he continued to protest when he made his Saturday telephone call home, still not mentioning the difficulty he was experiencing with the foreman. But it had several times crossed his mind that one Monday morning he wouldn't be there, waiting for the van to pick him up, that he'd had enough.

'What would you do though, Liam Pat?' Feeny asked in Bob's Dining Rooms, where at weekends he and Liam Pat often met for a meal.

'Go home.'

Feeny nodded; then he sighed and after a pause said it could come to that. He'd seen it before, a bullying foreman with a down on a young fellow he'd specially pick out.

'It's got so's I hate him.'

Again Feeny allowed a silence to develop. Then he said:

'They look down on us.'

'How d'you mean?'

'Any man with an Irish accent. The way things are.'

'You mean bombs and stuff?'

'I mean, you're breathing their air and they'd charge you for it. The first time I run into you, Liam Pat, weren't your friends saying they wouldn't serve you in another bar you went into?'

'The Hop Poles, that is. They won't serve you in your working clothes.'

Feeny leaned forward, over a plate of liver and potatoes. He lowered his voice to a whisper. 'They wash the ware twice after us. Plates, cups, a glass you'd take a drink out of. I was in a launderette one time and I offered a woman the machine after I'd done with it. "No, thanks," she said soon's I opened my mouth.'

Liam Pat had never had such an experience, but people weren't friendly. It was all right in the gang; it was all right when he went out with Rafferty and Noonan, or with Feeny. But people didn't smile, they didn't nod or say something when they saw you coming. The first woman he rented a room from was suspicious, always in the hall when he left the house, as if she thought he might be doing a flit with her belongings. In the place Feeny had found for him a man who didn't live there, whose name he didn't know, came round every Sunday morning and you paid him and he wrote out a slip. He never said anything, and Liam Pat used to wonder if he had some difficulty with speech. Although there was other people's food in the kitchen, and although there were footsteps on the stairs and sometimes overhead, in the weeks Liam Pat had lived there he never saw any of the other tenants, or heard voices. The curtains of one of the down-stairs rooms were always drawn over, which you could see from the outside and which added to the dead feeling of the house.

'It's the same the entire time,' Feeny said. 'Stupid as pigs. Can they write their names? You can see them thinking it.'

Huxter would say it straight out. 'Get your guts put into it,' Huxter shouted at Liam Pat, and once when something wasn't done to his liking he said there were more brains in an Irish turnip. 'Tow that bloody island out into the sea,' he said another time. A drop of their own medicine, he said.

'I couldn't get you shifted,' Feeny said. 'If I could I would.'

'Another gang, like?'

'Maybe in a couple of weeks there'd be something.'

'It'd be great, another gang.'

'Did you ever know McTighe?'

Liam Pat shook his head. He said Feeny had asked him that before. Did McTighe run a gang? he asked.

'He's in with a bookie. It'd be a good thing if you knew McTighe. Good all round, Liam Pat.'

*

Ten days later, when Liam Pat was drinking with Rafferty and Noonan in the Spurs and Horse, Feeny joined them and afterwards walked away from the public house with Liam Pat.

'Will we have one for the night?' he suggested, surprising Liam Pat because they'd come away when closing time was called and it would be the same anywhere else. 'No problem,' Feeny said, disposing at once of this objection.

'I have to get the last bus out, though. Ten minutes it's due.'

'You can doss where we're going. No problem at all, boy.'

He wondered if Feeny was drunk. He'd best get back to his bed, he insisted, but Feeny didn't appear to hear him. They turned into a side street. They went round to the back of a house. Feeny knocked gently on a window-pane and the rattle of television voices ceased almost immediately. The back door of the house opened.

'Here's Liam Pat Brogan,' Feeny said.

A bulky middle-aged man, with coarse fair hair above stolid, reddish features, stood in the rectangle of light. He wore a black jersey and trousers.

'The hard man,' he greeted Liam Pat, proffering a hand with a cut healing along the edge of the thumb.

'Mr McTighe,' Feeny completed his introduction. 'We were passing.'

Mr McTighe led the way into a kitchen. He snapped open two cans of beer and handed one to each of his guests. He picked up a third from the top of a refrigerator. Carling it was, Black Label.

'How're you doing, Liam Pat?' Mr McTighe asked.

Liam Pat said he was all right, but Feeny softly denied that. More of the same, he reported: a foreman giving an Irish lad a hard time. Mr McTighe made a sympathetic motion with his large, square head. He had a hoarse voice, that seemed to come from the depths of his chest. A Belfast man, Liam Pat said to himself when he got used to the accent, a city man.

'Is the room OK?' Mr McTighe asked, a query that came as a surprise. 'Are you settled?'

Liam Pat said his room was all right, and Feeny said:

'It was Mr McTighe fixed that for you.'

'The room?'

'He did of course.'

'It's a house that's known to me,' Mr McTighe said, and did not elucidate further. He gave a racing tip, Cassandra's Friend at Newton Abbot, the first race.

'Put your shirt on that, Liam Pat,' Feeny advised, and laughed. They stayed no more than half an hour, leaving the kitchen as they had entered it, by the door to the back yard. On the street Feeny said:

'You're in good hands with Mr McTighe.'

Liam Pat didn't understand that, but didn't say so. It would have something to do with the racing tip, he said to himself. He asked who the man who came round on Sunday mornings for the rent was.

'I wouldn't know that, boy.'

'I think I'm the only lodger there at the moment. There's a few shifted out, I'd say.'

'It's quiet for you so.'

'It's quiet all right.'

Liam Pat had to walk back to the house that night; there'd been no question of dossing down in Mr McTighe's. It took him nearly two hours, but the night was fine and he didn't mind. He went over the conversation that had taken place, recalling Mr McTighe's concern for his well-being, still bewildered by it. He slept soundly when he lay down, not bothering to take off his clothes, it being so late.

*

Weeks went by, during which Liam Pat didn't see Feeny. One of the other rooms in the house where he lodged was occupied again, but only for a weekend, and then he seemed once more to be on his own. One Friday Huxter gave Rafferty and Noonan their cards, accusing them of skiving. 'Stay if you want to,' he said to Liam Pat, and Liam Pat was aware that the foreman didn't want him to go, that he served a purpose as Huxter's butt. But without his friends he was lonely, and a bitter resentment continuously nagged him, spreading from the foreman's treatment of him and affecting with distortion people who were strangers to him.

'I think I'll go back,' he said the next time he ran into Feeny, outside the Spurs and Horse one night. At first he'd thought Feeny was touchy when he went on about his experience in a launderette or plates being washed twice; now he felt it could be true. You'd buy a packet of cigarettes off the same woman in a shop and she wouldn't pass a few minutes with you, even though you'd been in yesterday. The only good part of being in this city was the public houses where you'd meet boys from home, where there was a bit of banter and cheerfulness, and a sing-song when it was permitted. But when the evening was over you were on your own again.

'Why'd you go back, boy?'

'It doesn't suit me.'

'I know what you mean. I often thought of it myself.'

'It's no life for a young fellow.'

'They've driven you out. They spent eight centuries tormenting us and now they're at it again.'

'He called my mam a hooer.'

Huxter wasn't fit to tie Mrs Brogan's laces, Feeny said. He'd seen it before, he said. 'They're all the same, boy.'

'I'll finish out the few weeks with the job we're on.'

'You'll be home for Christmas.'

'I will.'

They were walking slowly on the street, the public houses emptying, the night air dank and cold. Feeny paused in a pool of darkness, beneath a street light that wasn't working. Softly, he said:

'Mr McTighe has the business for you.'

It sounded like another tip, but Feeny said no. He walked on in silence, and Liam Pat said to himself it would be another job, a different foreman. He thought about that. Huxter was the worst of it, but it wasn't only Huxter. Liam Pat was homesick for the estate, for the small town where people said hullo to you. Since he'd been here he'd eaten any old how, sandwiches he bought the evening before, for breakfast and again in the middle of the day, burger and chips later on, Bob's Dining Rooms on a Sunday. He hadn't thought about that before he'd come – what he'd eat, what a Sunday would be like. Sometimes at Mass he saw a girl he liked the look of, the same girl each time, quiet-featured, with her hair tied back. But when he went up to her after Mass a few weeks back she turned away without speaking.

'I don't want another job,' he said.

'Why would you, Liam Pat? After what they put you through?'

'I thought you said Mr McTighe –'

'Ah no, no. Mr McTighe was only remembering the time you and Dessie Coglan used distribute the little magazine.'

They still walked slowly, Feeny setting the pace.

'We were kids though,' Liam Pat said, astonished at what was being said.

'You showed your colours all the same.'

Liam Pat didn't understand that. He didn't know why they were talking about a time when he was still at the Brothers', when he and Dessie Coglan used to push the freedom magazine into the letter-boxes. As soon as it was dark they'd do it, so's no one would see them. Undercover stuff, Dessie used to say, and a couple of times he mentioned Michael Collins.

'I had word from Mr McTighe,' Feeny said.

'Are we calling in there?'

'He'll have a beer for us.'

'We were only being big fellas when we went round with the magazine.'

'It's remembered you went round with it.'

Liam Pat never knew where the copies of the magazine came from. Dessie Coglan just said the lads, but more likely it was the barber, Gaughan, an elderly man who lost the four fingers of his left hand in 1921. Liam Pat often noticed Dessie coming out of Gaughan's or talking to Gaughan in his doorway, beneath the striped barber's pole. In spite of his fingerless hand, Gaughan could still shave a man or cut a head of hair.

'Come on in,' Mr McTighe invited, opening his back door to them. 'That's a raw old night.'

They sat in the kitchen again. Mr McTighe handed round cans of Carling Black Label.

'You'll do the business, Liam?'

'What's that, Mr McTighe?'

'Feeny here'll show you the ropes.'

'The thing is, I'm going back to Ireland.'

'I thought maybe you would be. "There's a man will be going home," I said to myself. Didn't I say that, Feeny?'

'You did of course, Mr McTighe.'

'What I was thinking, you'd do the little thing for me before you'd be on your way, Liam. Like we were discussing the other night,' Mr McTighe said, and Liam Pat wondered if he'd had too much beer that night, for he couldn't remember any kind of discussion taking place.

*

Feeny opened the door of the room where the curtains were drawn over and took the stuff from the floorboards. He didn't switch the light on, but instead shone a torch into where he'd lifted away a section of the boards. Liam Pat saw red and black wires and the cream-coloured face of a timing device. Child's play, Feeny said, extinguishing the torch.

Liam Pat heard the floorboards replaced. He stepped back into the passage off which the door of the room opened.

Together he and Feeny passed through the hall and climbed the stairs to Liam Pat's room.

'Pull down that blind, boy,' Feeny said.

There was a photograph of Liam Pat's mother stuck under the edge of a mirror over a wash-basin; just above it, one of his father had begun to curl at the two corners that were exposed. The cheap brown suitcase he'd travelled from Ireland with was open on the floor, clothes he'd brought back from the launderette dumped in it, not yet sorted out. He'd bought the suitcase in Lacey's in Emmet Street, the day after he gave in his notice to O'Dwyer.

'Listen to me now,' Feeny said, sitting down on the bed.

The springs rasped noisily. Feeny put a hand out to steady the sudden lurch of the headboard. 'I'm glad to see that,' he said, gesturing with his head in the direction of a card Liam Pat's mother had made him promise he'd display in whatever room he found for himself. In the Virgin's arms the infant Jesus raised two chubby fingers in blessing.

'I'm not into anything like you're thinking,' Liam Pat said.

'Mr McTighe brought you over, boy.'

Feeny's wizened features were without expression. His priestly suit was shapeless, worn through at one of the elbows. A tie as narrow as a bootlace hung from the soiled collar of his shirt, its minuscule knot hard and shiny. He stared at his knees when he said Mr McTighe had brought Liam Pat from Ireland. Liam Pat said:

'I came over on my own though.'

Still examining the dark material stretched over his knees, as if fearing damage here also, Feeny shook his head.

'Mr McTighe fixed the room. Mr McTighe watched your welfare. "I like the cut of Liam Pat Brogan." Those were his words, boy. The day after yourself and myself went round to him the first time wasn't he on the phone to me, eight a.m. in the morning? Would you know what he said that time?'

'No, I wouldn't.'

' "We have a man in Liam Pat Brogan," was what he said.'

'I couldn't do what you're saying all the same.'

'Listen to me, boy. They have no history on you. You're no more than another Paddy going home for Christmas. D'you understand what I'm saying to you, Liam Pat?'

'I never heard of Mr McTighe till I was over here.'

'He's a friend to you, Liam Pat, the same way's I am myself. Haven't I been a friend, Liam Pat?'

'You have surely.'

'That's all I'm saying to you.'

'I'd never have the nerve for a bomber.'

'Sure, is there anyone wants to be? Is there a man on the face of God's earth would make a choice, boy?' Feeny paused. He took a handkerchief from a pocket of his trousers and passed it beneath his nose. For the first time since they'd entered Liam Pat's room he looked at him directly. 'There'll be no harm done, boy. No harm to life or limb. Nothing the like of that.'

Liam Pat frowned. He shook his head, indicating further bewilderment.

'Mr McTighe wouldn't ask bloodshed of anyone,' Feeny went on. 'A Sunday night. You follow me on that? A Sunday's a dead day in the city. Not a detail of that written down,

though. Neither date nor time. Nothing I'm saying to you.'
He tapped the side of his head. 'Nothing, only memorized.'

Feeny went on talking then. Because there was no chair in
the room, Liam Pat sat on the floor, his back to the wall.
Child's play, Feeny said again. He talked about Mr McTighe
and the mission that possessed Mr McTighe, the same that
possessed every Irishman worth his salt, the further from
home he was the more it was there. 'You understand me?'
Feeny said often, punctuating his long speech with this query,
concerned in case there was incomprehension where there
should be clarity. 'The dream of Wolfe Tone,' he said. 'The
dream of Isaac Butt and Charles Stewart Parnell. The dream
of Lord Edward Fitzgerald.'

The names stirred classroom memories for Liam Pat, the
lay teacher Riordan requesting information about them, his
bitten moustache disguising a long upper lip, a dust of chalk
on his pinstripes. 'Was your man Fitzgerald in the Flight of the
Earls?' Hasessy asked once, and Riordan was contemptuous.

'The massacre of the innocents,' Feeny said. 'Bloody Sunday.' He spoke of lies and deception, of falsity and broken
promises, of bullying that was hardly different from the
bullying of Huxter. 'O'Connell,' he said. 'Pearse. Michael
Collins. Those are the men, Liam Pat, and you'll walk away
one of them. You'll walk away ten feet high.'

As a fish is attracted by a worm and yet suspicious of it,
Liam Pat was drawn into Feeny's oratory. 'God, you could
be the Big Fella himself,' Dessie Coglan complimented him
one night when they were delivering the magazines. He had
seen the roadside cross that honoured the life and the death

of the Big Fella; he had seen the film only a few weeks back. He leaned his head against the wall and, while staring at Feeny, saw himself striding with Michael Collins's big stride. The torrent of Feeny's assurances and promises, and the connections Feeny made, affected him, but even so he said:

'Sure, someone could be passing though.'

'There'll be no one passing, boy. A Sunday night's chosen to make sure of it. Nothing only empty offices, no watchmen on the premises. All that's gone into.'

Feeny pushed himself off the bed. He motioned with his hand and Liam Pat stood up. Between now and the incident, Feeny said, there would be no one in the house except Liam Pat. Write nothing down, he instructed again. 'You'll be questioned. Policemen will maybe get on the train. Or they'll be at the docks when you get there.'

'What'll I say to them though?'

'Only that you're going home to County Cork for Christmas. Only that you were nowhere near where they're asking you about. Never in your life. Never heard of it.'

'Will they say do I know you? Will they say do I know Mr McTighe?'

'They won't have those names. If they ask you for names say the lads in your gang, say Rafferty and Noonan, say any names you heard in public houses. Say Feeny and McTighe if you're stuck. They won't know who you're talking about.'

'Are they not your names then?'

'Why would they be, boy?'

Liam Pat's protestation that he couldn't do it didn't weaken at first, but as Feeny went on and on, the words becoming images in Liam Pat's vision, he himself always at the centre of things, he became aware of an excitement. Huxter wouldn't know what was going to happen; Huxter would look at him and assume he was the same. The people who did not say hullo when he bought cigarettes or a newspaper would see no difference either. There was a strength in the excitement, a vigour Liam Pat had never experienced in his life before. He would carry the secret on to the site every morning. He would walk through the streets with it, a power in him where there'd been nothing. 'You have a Corkman's way with you,' Feeny said, and in the room with the drawn curtains he showed Liam Pat the business.

*

Sixteen days went by before the chosen Sunday arrived. In the Spurs and Horse during that time Liam Pat wanted to talk the way Feeny and Mr McTighe did, in the same soft manner, mysteriously, some private meaning in the words he used. He was aware of a lightness in his mood and confidence in his manner, and more easily than before he was drawn into conversation. One evening the barmaid eyed him the way Rosita Drudy used to eye Dessie Coglan years ago in Brady's Bar.

Liam Pat didn't see Feeny again, as Feeny had warned him he wouldn't. He didn't see Mr McTighe. The man didn't call for the rent, and for sixteen days Liam Pat was the only person in the house. He kept to his room except when he went to take up the sawn-through floorboards, familiarizing himself with what had to be done, making sure there was space enough in the sports bag when the clock was packed in a way that was convenient to set it. He cooked nothing in the kitchen because Feeny had said better not to. He didn't understand that, but even so he obeyed the command, thinking of it in that way, an order, no questions asked. He made tea in his room, buttering bread and sprinkling sugar on the butter, opening tins of beans and soup, eating the contents cold. Five times in all he made the journey he was to make on the chosen Sunday, timing himself as Feeny had suggested, becoming used to the journey and alert to any variations there might be.

On the Saturday before the Sunday he packed his suitcase and took it across the city to a locker at Euston Station, still following Feeny's instructions. When he returned to the house he collected what tins he'd opened and what food was left and filled a carrier bag, which he deposited in a dustbin in another street. The next day he had a meal at one o'clock in Bob's Dining Rooms, the last he would ever have there. The people were friendlier than they'd been before.

Nothing that belonged to him remained in his room, or in the house, when he left it for the last time. Feeny said to clean his room with the Philips cleaner that was kept for general use at the bottom of the stairs. He said to go over everywhere, all the surfaces, and Liam Pat did so, using the little round brush without any extension on the suction tube. For his own protection, that was. Wipe the handles of the doors with a tissue last thing of all, Feeny had advised, anywhere he might have touched.

Shortly after seven he practised the timing again. He

wanted to smoke a cigarette in the downstairs room, but he didn't because Feeny had said not to. He zipped up the sports bag and left the house with it. Outside, he lit a cigarette.

On the way to the bus stop, two streets away, he dropped the key of the house down a drain, an instruction also. When Feeny had been advising him about cleaning the surfaces and making sure nothing was left that could identify him, Liam Pat had had the impression that Mr McTighe wouldn't have bothered with any of that, that all Mr McTighe was interested in was getting the job done. He went upstairs on the bus and sat at the back. A couple got off at the next stop, leaving him on his own.

It was then that Liam Pat began to feel afraid. It was one thing to have it over Huxter, to know what Huxter didn't know; it was one thing to get a smile from the barmaid. It was another altogether to be sitting on a bus with a device in a sports bag. The excitement that had first warmed him while he listened to Feeny, while he sat on the floor with his head resting against the wall, wasn't there any more. Mr McTighe picking him out felt different now, and when he tried to see himself in Michael Collins's trenchcoat, with Michael Collins's stride, there was nothing there either. It sounded meaningless, Feeny saying he had a Corkman's way with him.

He sat with the sports bag on the floor, steadied by his feet on either side of it. A weakness had come into his arms, and for a moment he thought he wouldn't be able to lift them, but when he tried it was all right, even though the feeling of weakness was still there. A moment later nausea caused him to close his eyes.

The bus lurched and juddered through the empty Sunday-evening streets. Idling at bus stops, its engine vibrated, and between his knees Liam Pat's hand repeatedly reached down to seize the handles of the sports bag, steadying it further. He wanted to get off, to hurry down the stairs that were beside where he was sitting, to jump off the bus while it was still moving, to leave the sports bag where it was. He sensed what he did not understand: that all this had happened before, that his terror had come so suddenly because he was experiencing, again, what he had experienced already.

Two girls came chattering up the stairs and walked down the length of the bus. They laughed as they sat down, one of them bending forward, unable to control herself. The other went on with what she was saying, laughing too, but Liam Pat couldn't hear what she said. The conductor came for their fares and when he'd gone they found they didn't have a light for their cigarettes. The one who'd laughed so much was on the inside, next to the window. The other one got up. 'Ta,' she said when she had asked Liam Pat if he had a lighter and he handed her his box of matches. He didn't strike one because of the shaking in his hands, but even so she must have seen it. 'Ta,' she said again.

It could have been in a dream. He could have dreamed he was on a bus with the bag. He could have had a dream and forgotten it, like you sometimes did. The night he'd seen Feeny for the last time, it could have been he had a dream of being on a bus, and he tried to remember waking up the next morning, but he couldn't.

The girl next to the window looked over her shoulder, as

if she'd just been told that he'd handed her friend the box instead of striking a match for her. They'd remember him because of that. The one who'd approached him would remember the sports bag. 'Cheers,' the same one said when they both left the bus a couple of stops later.

It wasn't a dream. It was the *Examiner* spread out on the kitchen table a few months ago and his father shaking his head over the funeral, sourly demanding why those people couldn't have been left to their grief, why there were strangers there, wanting to carry the coffin. 'My God! My God!' his father savagely exclaimed.

It hadn't worked the first time. A Sunday night then too, another boy, another bus. Liam Pat tried to remember that boy's name, but he couldn't. 'Poor bloody hero,' his father said.

Another Dessie Coglan had done the big fella, fixing it, in touch with another Gaughan, in touch with the lads, who came to parade at the funeral. Another Huxter was specially picked. Another Feeny said there'd be time to spare to get to Euston afterwards, no harm to life or limb, ten exactly the train was. The bits and pieces had been scraped up from the pavement and the street, skin and bone, part of a wallet fifty yards away.

Big Ben was chiming eight when he got off the bus, carrying the sports bag slightly away from his body, although he knew that was a pointless precaution. His hands weren't shaking any more, the sickness in his stomach had passed, but still he was afraid, the same fear that had begun on the bus, cold in him now.

Not far from where Big Ben had sounded there was a bridge over the river. He'd crossed it with Rafferty and Noonan, his first weekend in London, when they'd thought they were going to Fulham only they got it all wrong. He knew which way to go, but when he reached the river wall he had to wait because there were people around, and cars going by. And when the moment came, when he had the bag on the curved top of the wall, another car went by and he thought it would stop and come back, that the people in it would know. But that car went on, and the bag fell with hardly a splash into the river, and nothing happened.

*

O'Dwyer had work for him, only he'd have to wait until March, until old Hoyne reached the month of his retirement. Working the mixer it would be again, tarring roofs, sweeping the yard at the end of the day. He'd get on grand, O'Dwyer said. Wait a while and you'd never know; wait a while and Liam Pat could be his right-hand man. There were no hard feelings because Liam Pat had taken himself off for a while.

'Keep your tongue to yourself,' Mrs Brogan had warned her husband in a quiet moment the evening Liam Pat so unexpectedly returned. It surprised them that he had come the way he had, a roundabout route when he might have come the way he went, the Wexford crossing. 'I missed the seven train,' he lied, and Mrs Brogan knew he was lying because she had that instinct with her children. Maybe something to do with a girl, she imagined, his suddenly coming back. But she left that uninvestigated, too.

'Ah sure, it doesn't suit everyone,' Dessie Coglan said in Brady's Bar. Any day now it was for Rosita and he was full of that. He never knew a woman get pregnant as easy as Rosita, he said. He didn't ask Liam Pat if he'd used the telephone number he'd given him, if that was how he'd got work. 'You could end up with fourteen of them,' he said. Rosita herself was one of eleven.

Liam Pat didn't say much, either to O'Dwyer or at home or to Dessie Coglan. Time hung heavy while old Hoyne worked out the few months left of his years with O'Dwyer. Old Hoyne had never risen to being more than a general labourer, and Liam Pat knew he never would either.

He walked out along the Mountross road every afternoon, the icy air of a bitterly cold season harsh on his hands and face. Every day of January and a milder February, going by the rusted gates of Mountross Abbey and the signpost to Ballyfen, he thought about the funeral at which there'd been the unwanted presence of the lads, and sometimes saw it as his own.

All his life he would never be able to tell anyone. He could never describe that silent house or the stolid features of Mr McTighe or repeat Feeny's talk. He could never speak of the girls on the bus, how he hadn't been able to light a match, or how so abruptly he realized that this was the second attempt. He could never say that he'd stood with the sports bag on the river wall, that nothing had happened when it struck the water. Nor that he cried when he walked away, that tears ran down his cheeks and on to his clothes, that he cried for the bomber who might have been himself.

He might have left the bag on the bus, as he had thought he would. He might have hurried down the stairs and jumped off quickly. But in his fear he had found a shred of courage and it had to do with the boy: he knew that now and could remember the feeling. It was his mourning of the boy, as he might have mourned himself.

On his walks, and when he sat down to his meals, and when he listened to his parents' conversation, the mourning was still there, lonely and private. It was there in Brady's Bar and in the shops of the town when he went on his mother's messages. It would be there when again he took charge of a concrete-mixer for O'Dwyer, when he shovelled wet cement and worked in all weathers. On the Mountross road Liam Pat didn't walk with the stride of Michael Collins, but wondered instead about the courage his fear had allowed, and begged that his mourning would not ever cease.

A Friend in the Trade

They fell in love when *A Whiter Shade of Pale* played all summer. They married when Tony Orlando sang *Tie a Yellow Ribbon Round the Old Oak Tree*. These tunes are faded memories now, hardly there at all, and they've forgotten Procol Harum and Suzi Quatro and Brotherhood of Man, having long ago turned to Brahms.

The marriage has managed well, moving with ease through matrimony's stages, weathering its storms. It seems absurd to Clione when she looks back that she fussed so because at their first dinner party her husband of a month innocently remarked that she hadn't made the profiteroles herself. It was ridiculous in turn, James has apologized, that he banged out of the house when coffee was spilt over Pedbury's *The Optimistic Gardener*, ridiculous that he had not been calm when they missed the night train at the Gare de Lyon, ridiculous that they'd rowed about it when the workmen laid the wrong tiles.

The intensity of passion, and touchiness surfacing quickly, gave way to familial pleasure and familial pressures – three children growing up, their grandparents growing old. Tranquillity came when the children grew up a little more, when a Sunset Home took in a grandfather, a Caring Fold a grandmother. Give and take ruled the middle years; the marriage took on the odds and won. Passed through the battle, surviving dog days' ennui, love now seems surer than before.

Clione is still as slender as ever she was, with wide blue eyes that still, occasionally, have a startled look. Beauty has not finished with her: her delicately made features – straight classic nose and sculptured lips – are as they always were, and cobweb wrinkles have an attraction of their own. She is glad she did not marry someone else and could not ever have considered being unfaithful. She knows – she doesn't have to ask – that her husband has not been faithless either.

He deals in first editions and manuscripts. As well, he and Clione run the Asterisk Press together, publishing the verse of poets who are in fashion, novellas, short stories, from time to time a dozen or so pages of reminiscence by a writer whose standing guarantees the interest of collectors. Their business is conducted from home, an old suburban house in south-west London, not far from the river. Provincial auctions are attended in pursuit of forgotten tomes and the letters of the literati, alive or dead. The demands of the Asterisk Press – the choosing of typefaces and bindings, paper of just the right shade and weight, mail-order sales – provide a contrast. A catalogue that combines both sources of livelihood is published every six months or so.

Years ago, the trade in first editions and other rarities threw up Michingthorpe, who specializes mainly in what he calls nineteenth-century jottings. A 'trade friend' James calls him, but there is more to it than this designation implies. Since before the children were born, before the funerals of the grandparents, Michingthorpe has been a regular presence in the house near the river. He has brought with him the excitement of jottings that are special; a discovery that defies or contradicts the agreed opinion of academe delights him most of all. But anything will do, for everything is special, or becomes so in Michingthorpe's possession. Scraps of letters are lovingly laid out; the beginning of a Dickens chapter that was not proceeded with; frustrated Coleridge lines, scratched out, begun again; a note to a tailor; initials on a bill. All have been offered to James and Clione for perusal and admiration.

Michingthorpe talks mostly about himself. In remarking on the particular way a great Victorian author had of looping his l's or y's, he manages to make the matter personal to himself, going on to relate that he loops his own letters in that way too, or does not. Responding to a comment or prediction about the weather, he recalls how when he was in Venice once – on the track of a John Cross jotting – rain for six days caused the canals to rise, trapping him in his hotel with nothing better to re-read than Chesterton's life of Browning, which he had not cared for the first time. If frost is forecast, he recalls that it brings on an ailment. He had an uncle who perished in a storm, struck by the bough of a cherry tree.

Michingthorpe was already running to youthful fat when he first became a trade friend; he is fatter now. The flesh that smudges the contours of his face is pale. Eyes, behind spectacles, are slate-coloured and small. His hair was conventionally short when he was younger; now its grey mat obscures his ears in so distinctive a manner that Clione has heard her waggish son likening Michingthorpe to a New Testament disciple. Had Michingthorpe himself heard that, he would not have minded but possibly would have recalled that as a schoolboy he wrote an essay on the subject of the Last Supper and was awarded a prize for it. He welcomes it when he is spoken of, adverse comments being rarely recognized as such.

When her middle child was three years old, Clione came into the sitting-room one day to hear Michingthorpe explaining why it was that oysters did not agree with him. He recounted occasions, before he was aware that they did not, when disaster had occurred. Still on the subject of his digestion, he next spoke of a dressmaker who had taken a liking to him in his own childhood, always having rock buns ready when he called in to see her. The rock buns had no ill effects, even though on one occasion he had eaten seven. Changing the subject, though without alteration of expression or tone, he reported that when he first wore spectacles everything tilted – whole rooms, and lamp-posts, the pavement when he walked on it. This led to a memory of someone saying, 'We see God's world as God would wish us to.' Once in a zoo he watched a gorilla escape. He recognized on the street one day the late Boris Karloff. Often he speaks of waiters – how skilled or careless one was last week, what he had eaten on that occasion, whose company he was in. His mealtime companions are always from the trade, business conducted over soup and entrée and pudding.

In the past Michingthorpe appeared to dress more ordinarily: clothes that were hardly noticeable in youth – jeans and T-shirts – are more emphatic with his long grey hair, as if they seek to make a point or perpetuate some illusion. There are chunky jerseys to go with them, horn buttons down the front.

'I dare say we all are someone else's unpresentable friend,' Clione has said, causing her husband and children to laugh, because Clione herself is not in the least unpresentable.

The children, who are adults now – the waggish boy, two younger girls – have ages ago come to regard Michingthorpe as they do the familiar items of furniture in their parents' house. He is something that has been there for as long as the buttoned sofa in the hall has been, and the ugly picture of mules drawing carts on the stairway wall, the davenport on the first-floor landing. For all the children's lives he has come and gone, expected or not expected, some detail at once related about the journey he has made. 'Oh, God, that man!' the children have cried, when young, when older. Not that Michingthorpe has ever noticed them much, seeming not ever to have established which is which. Among themselves they still wonder, as they always have, how it is that he continues to be a welcome visitor in their parents' house. The fact bewilders them, but then is packed away as one of the small mysteries that haunt the separation of generations.

The children are visitors themselves now, coming back to the house when they are ill or unhappy in a love affair, though often leaving again without mentioning anything; or coming back because they are, all three, affectionately disposed towards both their mother and their father. Their mother's fifty-first birthday draws them for Sunday lunch one damp February weekend, the last time it will be celebrated in this house, for after nearly twenty-five years there is to be a move. 'We rattle about like two ageing peas,' Clione has said, 'now that you have left us on our own.' Two days ago an offer was made for a converted oast-house in Sussex. Tomorrow it will be known if it has been accepted.

Clione has privately resolved that if it isn't she'll somehow find the extra and pay the asking price. Her childhood was passed in the country, and already she has wondered about keeping a dog – a spaniel – as once she did. Time has been on her hands since her children's going; she wants to grow her own vegetables again, to have asparagus beds, to cosset anemones and clematis and hellebores. Some intuition tells her she'll delight in that.

This prospect cheers Clione after her children have left, all together in the late afternoon, and the house in which all of them were born has gone quiet again. She wears a dress she bought specially for her birthday lunch, two shades of green, a silk scarf with an ivy pattern at her throat. Her presents clutter the sitting-room and there are torn cardboard packages on the floor, four different kinds of shiny coloured paper waiting to be folded: at Christmas it can be used again. Her cards are on the mantelpiece. A Rösel pepper-grinder is on the hearthrug beside her where she kneels, her new yellow coffee-maker on the armchair she usually sits in, Mahler's Sixth Symphony on disc beside it. The glow of smokeless fuel throws back a little heat at her.

Clione misses her children. It is missing them that drew

her to the oast-house, to thoughts of vegetables and plants. And the chances are that her children will be drawn to it too, that they'll come there more often than to the house in London, that they'll delight in the summer countryside and weekend walks about the lanes, in winter bleakness, the trees skeletal, brown empty hedges. She longs for her children sometimes, wanting to set the time back to when there were children's worries, so very easy to comfort, to when her children gave her what a husband can't, not even the most generous. That a child was stillborn is never spoken of by James or by herself; their living children do not know.

She pushes away a surge of melancholy and thinks again about the changing seasons in a garden that does not yet quite exist, about fitting in all the paraphernalia of the Asterisk Press in the upstairs rooms. No longer kneeling, she leans back against the seat of an armchair, her legs slipped more comfortably to one side. Her eyelids droop.

*

There is something about Michingthorpe's way of ringing a doorbell that indicates, in this house at least, who it is: a single short ring, shorter than most people's and never repeated. Michingthorpe knows the sound can be heard in all the rooms, that if the summons is not answered no one is in, even though some lights are on.

Her doze disturbed, Clione imagines him already in the room and bearing, as her children have, a brightly wrapped gift. The unlikely, sleepy fantasy goes on a little longer. She sees herself in gratitude embracing Michingthorpe – which

95

she has never done – and hears her voice exclaiming over what their visitor has brought.

Dusk is giving way to darkness. She shovels more coal on to the fire, then pulls the curtains over all three windows. The hall door bangs downstairs. Minutes later, in his long black overcoat, Michingthorpe is giftless in the sitting-room doorway.

'I knew of course that it was there.' He speaks to the air, as he always does, addressing no one. 'The funeral two months ago, disposal of the library on the eighth. They'd no idea. All that stuff and they'd no idea. I had the pickings to myself.'

He doesn't take his overcoat off. He has a way of sometimes not doing that. He sits down, still talking, saying he spent the night before in the temperance hotel of the town he visited, the only hotel there was. He and a local bookseller were the only dealers, and all the bookseller wanted was the Hardy. Sluggish on the sofa, Michingthorpe polishes his glasses and carefully replaces them as he speaks.

'Frightful journey. Change twice and a tree down on the line at Immington. Of course I had the Grossmith stuff to annotate.'

Pouring drinks, James nods. His fair hair has gone nondescript and is receding; in fawn corduroy trousers, checked winter shirt, fawn pullover, he is a little stooped.

'Clione's birthday,' he says, offering Michingthorpe a Kir.

But nothing that is outside himself, or part of other people, ever influences Michingthorpe. His surface runs deep, for greater knowledge of him offers nothing more than what initially it presents. Roaming the Internet is his hobby, he sometimes says.

Still feeling a little woozy from the wine at lunchtime, Clione shakes her head at the offer of a drink and tidies the room instead. Michingthorpe says he has formed the opinion that Conrad conducted a correspondence with a woman called Rosa Hoogwerf.

'Then residing in Argentina, though why remains a mystery. I've floated the name on the Net.'

Clione wonders if he noticed that she has carried a yellow coffee-maker across the room, or registers that she is now gathering up the remains of cardboard packages from the floor. She clears away the birthday cards from the mantelpiece.

'Some woman in Hungary,' Michingthorpe is saying. 'By the sound of her, Rosa Hoogwerf's granddaughter.'

He has accepted the drink that has been poured for him, and Clione wonders why he is here, then realizes it is to tell about the journey he has made and the prize that has come his way. Someone who once visited his flat saw the refrigerator open, with only a single bottle of milk in it, and uncooked sausages on a plate and butter still in its foil. Michingthorpe is unmarried, has apparently never had with anyone – man or woman – what could be called a relationship. That is generally assumed, but assumed with confidence, and is not contradicted by the known facts.

Clione sits down again. The conversation dims to a grey murmur she doesn't listen to. She doesn't dislike Michingthorpe, she never has; he isn't an enemy of any kind. Sometimes she considers he isn't even a bore, simply a presence with small slate eyes and teenager's hair that has a biblical look. She isn't aware of how she knows he loves her.

'Not that I feel my age,' she suddenly hears now, and wonders if he has finally acknowledged that there has been a birthday in the house and has said when his is, in August, as he has said before. 'Miskolc is where that woman is. She has a little English.'

He has never, that Clione can remember, met her eye, for he doesn't go in for that with anyone; yet still she knows. For several years – and before, for she senses that it has been longer – there has been something that even now seems extraordinary: it is incredible that Michingthorpe can love anyone; incredible too that he can be mysterious. Burning the cardboard she has collected, continuing not to listen to what is said, she wonders yet again if he is aware that she senses his attachment.

'We can sell the house at last.'

She hears James passing this information on and looks to see the vagueness it inspires in Michingthorpe's plump features, as happens when something utterly without interest requires his attention.

'We've found an oast-house,' she says herself.

There is a different reaction now. For the first time in Clione's entire acquaintance with him, Michingthorpe allows his mouth to open in what appears to be shock. Nor does it close. His small eyes stare harshly at the air. He sits completely still, one hand grasping the other, both pressed into his chest.

'This is the country?'

'Well, yes. Sussex.'

There is a pause, and then recovery. Michingthorpe stands up. 'Originally my family came from Sussex. But a long time ago. Michingthorpe Ales.'

'We shall miss you.' Clione notices herself sounding as mischievous as one of her children. There is no protestation that they'll be missed themselves. For a long moment their empty-handed visitor is silent. But before he goes there's more about the Internet.

*

Pouring coffee at breakfast five days later, Clione waits to hear the content of an early-morning telephone call: only Michingthorpe gets in touch at five to eight. It has occasionally been earlier.

'He has been to see it.'

'What? Seen what?'

'The oast-house. He's been down there. Well, he was near, I think. Anyway, he has looked it over.'

'But why on earth?'

'It's decidedly unlike him, but even so he has. I think I told him where it was. Not that he asked.'

'You mean, he went along and bothered those people for no reason?'

'He just said he'd looked it over.'

A flicker of unease disturbs Clione. It might have amused her if ever she had confessed that Michingthorpe has feelings for her; but to have confessed as well that he has never displayed them, that her woman's intuition comes in here, would have led too easily on to a territory of embarrassment.

Could it all not be imagination on her part? Or put more cruelly, a fading beauty's yearning for attention? 'Oh, but surely,' Clione has heard James's objection, the amusement all his now. Better just to leave it, she has always considered.

'He knows our offer has been accepted?'

'Oh, yes, he knows.'

Two days later, in the early afternoon, they visit again the house they have bought, received there by an elderly man – a Mr Witheridge whom they have not met before, whose daughter and son-in-law showed them around. They are permitted to take measurements, and in whispers speak of structural changes they hope to make.

'Nice that your friend liked it too,' the old man says, waiting downstairs with teacups on a tray when they have finished.

Profuse apologies are offered, and explanations that sound lame. Some silly muddle, James vaguely mutters.

'Oh, good heavens, no! Oast-houses are in Mr Michingthorpe's family, it seems. Michingthorpe Ales, he mentioned.'

The garden is little more than a field with a few shrubs in it. The present occupants came in 1961; Mr Witheridge moved in when his wife died. All this is talked about over cups of tea, and how mahonias do well, and winter heathers. But there are no heathers, of any season, that Clione and James can see, and herbs have failed in brick-edged beds in the cobbled yard.

'Martins nest every year but they aren't a nuisance,' the old man assures them. 'I'd stay here for ever, actually.' He nods, then shrugs away his wish. 'But we need to be nearer to things. Not that we're entirely cut off. No, I don't want to go at all.'

'We're sorry to take it from you.' James smiles, again apologetic.

'Oh, good heavens, no! It's just that it's a happy place and we want you to be happy here, too. There's a bus that goes by regularly at the bottom of the lane. I explained that to your friend when he said he didn't drive.'

'Yes, I dare say he'll visit us.' Clione laughs, but doubts – and notices James doubting it too – that Michingthorpe often will, not being the country kind. The long acquaintanceship seems already over, the geography of their lives no longer able to contain it.

'Your friend was interested in the outhouses.'

*

'You're intending to live with us?' Clione stares into the puffy features, but the slaty eyes are blank, as everything else is. His voice is no more lifeless than it usually is when he explains that he happened to be in the neighbourhood of the oast-house, a library he had to look over at Nettleton Court.

'Not fifteen minutes away. Nothing of interest. A wasted journey, I said to myself, and that I hate.'

'You mentioned converting the outhouses to that old man.'

'I have a minikin's lifestyle. I like a certain smallness, I like things tidy around me. I throw things out, I do not keep possessions by me. That's always been my way, I've been quite noted for it.'

'We've no intention of converting the outhouses.'

Michingthorpe does not respond. He takes his spectacles off and looks at them, holding them far away. He puts them on again and says:

'What d'you think I got for the Madox Ford? Remember the Madox Ford?'

'We've never talked about your living with us.'

It is impossible to know if this is acknowledged, if there is a slight gesture of the head. Michingthorpe Ales were brewed at Maresfield, Clione learns, but that was long ago. In the 1730s, then for a generation or two.

'I never took much interest. Just chance that I stumbled across the family name. In Locke's *Provincial Byeways*, I believe it was.'

'We'll move down there in May.'

Quite badly foxed, the Ford, the frontispiece gone. 'Well, you saw yourself. Six five, would you have thought it?'

*

Later, Clione passes all that on. The faint unease she experienced when she heard that Michingthorpe had been to Sussex is greater now. For more than twenty years he has had the freedom of a household, been given the hospitality a cat which does not belong to it is given, or birds that come to a window-sill. Has he seen all this as something else? It seems to Clione that it must be so, that what appears to her children and her husband to have come out of the blue is a projection of what was there already. Michingthorpe's clumsy presumption is the presumption of an innocent, which is what his unawareness makes him. She should say that, but finds she cannot.

She listens to family laughter and when the children are no longer there says she is to blame, that she should have anticipated that something like this would one day happen.

'Of course you're not to blame.'

'It was my fault that he presumed so.'

'I don't see how.'

She tells because at last she has to, because what didn't matter matters now. A misunderstanding, she calls it. She knew and she just left it there, permitting it.

'Oh, but surely this can't be so? Surely not?'

'I've always thought of it as harmless.'

'You couldn't have imagined it?'

She does not let a stab of anger show. Her husband is smiling at her, standing by the windows of the sitting-room they soon will leave for ever. His smile is kind. He is not mocking or being a tease.

'No, I haven't imagined it.'

'Poor bloody fool!'

'Yes.'

She does not confess that after her recent conversation with Michingthorpe she felt sorry she'd been cold, that bewilderingly she dreamed these last few nights of his shadow thrown on snow that had fallen in the oast-house garden, his shadow on sunlit grass, an imprecise reflection in a pool on the cobbles where the outhouses were. His fleshy palms were warmed by a coffee mug while his talk went on, while she beat up a soufflé, while again he recalled the dressmaker who had made him rock buns.

'It's horrid,' she says. 'Dropping someone.'

'I know.'

James does know; she is aware of that, drawn into his thoughts, as their closeness so often allows. Dropping someone is not in James's nature, yet why should they pander to the awkward selfishness of an oddity? There are the memories that go back to *A Whiter Shade of Pale*, the settlements and compromises of the marriage they were determined to make work. Her friends have not always been her husband's kind, nor his hers, and there were other differences that, with time, didn't matter either. The intimacy they have come to know is like a growth of roots, spreading and entangling, making them almost one. Why should there be embarrassment now?

'For it would be like that,' she hears James say. 'Day after day.'

'He has a nothing life.'

She pleads before she knows she's doing so, and realizes then that she has done so before. In the car when they drove away after the revelation in the oast-house she suggested that the old man might have misheard, that it was probably gratuitous information on his part about the buses passing near, not the answer to a question. You can pity a child, Clione finds herself thinking, no matter what a child is like.

'It's a different kind of love,' she murmurs, hesitating over every word.

'It's fairly preposterous, whatever it is.'

'For all the time we've known him we have looked after him. You as much as I.'

'My dear, we can't play fantasies with a fully grown man.'

She sees again the shadow from her dream, distorted when it crosses the cobbles from the outhouses, cast bulkily on the kitchen floor, taking sunlight from the table spread with her cooking things. Being a shadow suits him, as being a joke once did.

'It was just a thought he had,' she says.

*

On a cool May morning, piece by piece, the furniture is carried across the pavement to the removal vans. The men are given cups of tea, the doors of the vans are closed. Clione passes from one room to the next through the emptiness of the house where her three children were born, the house in which they grew up and then left, leaving her too. Who will listen to him now? Who'll watch him talking to the air? Who'll not want to know what a splendid find he has come across at another auction? Who'll not want to know that oysters don't agree with him?

He is there when they drive off but does not wave, as if already he does not know them, as if he never did. 'Oh, he'll latch on to someone else,' the children have said, each of them putting it in that same way. 'He won't mind your going much.' She cannot guess how he'll mind, what form his minding will take, where or how the pain will be. But the pain is there, for she can feel it.

Their unpresentable friend won't come, not even once. Because he does not drive, because there is no point in it, because the pain would be too much. She does not know why he will not come, only that he won't. She does not know why the pity she feels is so intensely there, only that it is and that his empty love is not absurd.

Low Sunday, 1950

She put the wine in the sun, on the deep white window-sill, the bottle not yet opened. It cast a flush of red on the window-sill's surface beside the porcelain figure of a country girl with a sheaf of corn, the only ornament there. It felt like a celebration, wine laid out to catch the last of the warmth on a Sunday evening, and Philippa wondered if her brother could possibly have forgotten what Sunday it was when he brought the bottle back from Findlater's on Friday.

There was no sound in the house. Upstairs, Tom would be reading. At this time of day at weekends he always read for a while, as she remembered him so often as a child, comfortable in the only armchair his bedroom contained. He had been tidier in the armchair then, legs tucked beneath him, body curled around his book; now the legs that had grown longer sprawled, spilt out from the cushions, while one arm dangled, a cigarette smouldering from the fingers that also turned the pages.

Philippa was petite by comparison, fair-haired, her quiet features grave in repose, a prettiness coming with animation. She took care with her clothes rather than dressed well. Her blouse today was two striped shades of green, one matching her skirt, the other her tiny emerald earrings. She was thirty-nine in the Spring of 1950, her brother three years older.

They did not regret, either of them, the fruits of the revolution that by chance had changed their lives in making them its casualties. They rejoiced in all that had come about and even took pride in their accidental closeness to the revolution as it had happened. They had been in at a nation's birth, had later experienced its childhood years, unprosperous and ordinary and undramatic. That a terrible beauty had transformed the land they had not noticed.

In the garden Philippa picked lily tulips and bluebells, and sprigs of pink hazel. Tom's vegetable beds were raked and marked to indicate where his seeds had not yet come up, but among the herbs the tarragon was sprouting, and apple mint, and lovage. Chives were at their best, sage thickening with soft fresh growth. Next weekend, he'd said, they should weed the long border, turn up the caked soil.

On the long wooden draining-board in the kitchen she began to arrange the flowers in two vases. Tom always bought the wine in Findlater's, settling the single bottle into the basket strapped to the handlebars of his bicycle. They didn't make much of Sunday lunch – a way of arranging the day that went back to their Aunt Adelaide's lifetime – and only on Sundays was there ever wine at supper. In the other house – before Philippa and her brother had come to Rathfarnham – decanters of whiskey and sherry had stood on the dining-room sideboard, regularly replenished, not there for appearance's sake. 'What you need's a quick one,' her father had said on the Sunday of which today was yet another anniversary, and poor little Joe Paddy hadn't been able to say anything in response, shivering from head to toe as if he had the flu. 'What d'you say to a sharpener?' had been another way of putting it – when Mr Tyson or Mr Higgins came to the house – or sometimes, 'Will we take a ball of malt?' When the outside walls were repainted, the work complete, the men packing up their brushes and their ladders, they had been brought in to have glasses filled at the sideboard. A credit to Sallymount Avenue, her father had said, referring to the work that had been done, and the glasses were raised to it.

'Well, I've finished that,' Tom said, knowing where to find her.

'What happened?'

'She married the naval fellow.'

'They'll manage.'

'Of course.'

She felt herself watched. Clipping the stems to the length she wanted each, shaping the hazel, she heard the rattle of his matches and knew if she turned her head she would see cigarettes and matches in one hand, the ashtray in the other. Players he smoked, though once it had been Woodbines, what he could afford then. 'You've been smoking, Tom!' Aunt Adelaide used to cry, exasperated. 'Tom, you are *not* to smoke!'

He came further in to the kitchen, tipped the ashtray into the waste bucket beneath the sink, washed it under the tap and put it aside to carry back upstairs later.

'Where's the old dog?' he asked. 'Come back, has he?'

She shook her head and then, together, they heard their dog in the garden, the single bark that indicated his return from the travels they could not control. She glanced up, through the window above the sink, and there he was, panting on the grass, a black and white terrier, his smooth coat wringing wet.

'He's been in the Dodder,' she said. 'Or somewhere.'

'He'll be the death of me, that dog.'

The word could be used; they neither of them flinched. It had a different resonance when applied so lightly to the boldness of their dog. Different again when encountered in lines of poetry. Even the Easter Passion – recently renewed for both of them in the Christ Church service on Good Friday evening – gave death a hallowed meaning, and softened it through the miracle of the Resurrection. But death as it had affected their lives was still raw, the moment of its awful pain still terrible if they let it have its way.

'I'll be an hour or so,' Tom said.

He scolded the exhausted dog on the lawn, and the dog was sheepish, hunching himself in shame and only daring then to wag his tail. Philippa watched from the window and guessed – and was right – that, exhaustion or not, Tom would be accompanied on his walk.

'No hurry.' She unlatched the window to call out, to smile because she realized, quite suddenly, that she hadn't during their conversation. This year she would go, she thought. She would go, and Tom would live his life.

*

Rathfarnham had hardly changed in all the years he'd known it; that was yet to come. This evening no one was about, the few small shops closed, the Yellow House – where he sometimes had a drink on weekdays – not open either. Low in the sky, the sun cast shadows that were hardly there.

'We're invited to Rathfarnham for tea,' Tom remembered his mother so often announcing in Sallymount Avenue, her tone reflecting the pleasure she knew the news would bring. The tram and then the long walk, for which it had to be fine or else, at the last minute, they wouldn't go. 'Oh, Aunt Adelaide'll know why,' their mother would say, and it was always only a postponement. Twice, Tom remembered, that happened, but probably there had been another time, now forgotten. The great spread on the dining-room table, the mysterious house – for it was mysterious then – were what the pleasure of those announcements had been about. Aunt Adelaide made egg sandwiches and sardine sandwiches, and two kinds of cake – fruit and sponge – and there were little square buns already buttered, and scones with raisins in them. In the garden, among the laurels, there was a secret place.

Perfectly obedient now, the dog trotted without a sign of weariness, as close to Tom's legs as he could manage. 'Well, wasn't that a grand day, sir?' an old man Tom didn't know remarked, and the dog went to sniff his trousers. 'Oh, I've seen you about all right,' the old man said, patting the black head.

What a *bouleversement* it had been in Aunt Adelaide's life! In a million years she couldn't have guessed that the two children who had occasionally come to tea, who had crept about upstairs, opening doors they knew they should not, who had whispered and pretended in the laurels, would every day and every night be there, her house their home, all mystery gone. Often on his weekend walks Tom thought about that; often on his return he and Philippa shared the remorse those thoughts engendered. How careless they had been of the imposition, how casual, how thoughtless! 'I shall have to lie down,' Aunt Adelaide used to say and Nelly, her maid and her companion, would angrily explain that that was because of rowdiness or some quarrel there had been. Murphy, who did the garden, who came every day – there being no shortages in Aunt Adelaide's spinster life – told them the blackly moustached figure, silver-framed on the drawing-room window-table, stern and unsmiling, was an admirer of long ago. They'd often wondered who he was.

Tom's sister had been wrong in assuming he could not possibly have forgotten what this Sunday was when he bought the wine. Tom had forgotten because, he supposed, he wanted to; dismounting from his bicycle outside Findlater's on Friday evening, he had been thinking of their summer holiday and so the aberration had occurred. Within a minute he had realized, but would have felt foolish handing the bottle back, and when he reached the house he felt it would have been underhand not to have brought the wine to the kitchen, as he always did if he'd bought a bottle. There had of course been Philippa's surprise, but it was natural between them that they did not comment.

When he had passed the last short terrace of cottages before he reached the countryside, Tom softly sang the first few lines of 'She is Far from the Land'. The song always came to him in the territory of the lovers it celebrated; here it was that Robert Emmet and Sarah Curran had walked too. Far ahead of him, the last of the sun no longer brightened the gorse on the slopes of Kilmashogue, where their stifled romance had been a happiness. Fiery, handsome Robert Emmet, foolish insurgent; gentle Sarah. In their company, Tom thought of them as friends – here or in the deerpark below the distant gorse slopes. They had sat in its summerhouse, talking of Ireland as it would one day be, and of themselves, how they'd be too. They had wandered in the future, as Tom now wandered in the past to eavesdrop in pretence. Part of today it was, the walk and being with them.

He lit a cigarette. In loving because she could not help herself, Sarah too had been a casualty of chance, beyond the battlefield yet left to bear the agony of scars you could not see. They hanged defiant Robert Emmet.

This past filled Tom's reflections as he walked on. If beauty had come to Ireland, tranquillity was its form: a quietness in Ireland's dark, a haven these lovers had not known. His pity was for them.

*

Philippa set the table, spreading first the bleached linen tablecloth. It had come from the house in Sallymount Avenue, as the extra knives and forks had, and the Galway glasses, and the table in the hall. But anything large – the dining-table with the leaves that could be added, the dining chairs, the carpets, the wardrobes, the sideboard – had had to go for auction because their aunt's rooms were on the crowded side already. 'A mistake,' Aunt Adelaide called what had happened, as if offering that as a consolation, since there was nothing else. Often she repeated it in that same way, and she would repeat it, too, when some visitor came, someone new to the district or from the far-off past: an explanation for the presence of two children in her house. 'A terrible mistake.'

Sausages they were having, Hafner's of course, which Philippa had gone specially in for yesterday, saying she had things to do in Henry Street. Sausages and mashed potatoes, and glazed carrots, which recently she had learned how to do. Then steamed fig pudding, which had been steaming for an hour already, and custard. Often Philippa wondered how it would be different, cooking for a husband. She sensed it would be, as she sensed Tom's return to the house every day would be different, but she did not know how. 'He's more than a brother to her,' their aunt had always lowered her voice to inform a visitor. 'Well, being older, of course.'

She made up mustard, mixing it in the small blue glass that lined the silver container. They'd listened at the banisters when Joe Paddy came knocking wildly at the door. Supposed to be in bed, they crouched there, and their father said what Joe Paddy needed was a drink, Joe Paddy shouting all the while that a man was after him, their mother calming him, saying the Troubles were all over now. He'd been in himself to see, their father said: Dublin had gone quiet after the carnage. He had stood and seen the surrender in the name of peace; there was nothing to be frightened of now. But Joe Paddy kept saying a man was after him.

She pricked the sausages and laid them on the fat that had gone liquid in the pan. 'If the man comes we'll explain to him,' their mother said. 'We'll explain you weren't in any of it, Joe Paddy.' And then the voices became murmurs, passing from the hall. She was asleep when there was shouting in the garden and she couldn't remember what anything was about. They went to the window to look out and there the man was, in a soldier's uniform. 'We'll explain,' their mother repeated, in the hall again. 'You stay where you are, boy,' their father said. 'You take another drink.'

The sausages fried slowly. She put the potatoes on. Tom would mash them when they were ready, and add a butter pat and chives. 'I'm going to try for the Bank of Ireland,' Tom had said, pleasing Aunt Adelaide because their father, too, had tried for the Bank of Ireland, and been employed for all his adult life in the architectural splendour of the College Green office, as Tom was now. 'You'll have the house, of course,' Aunt Adelaide had said, months before she died.

From the kitchen window Philippa saw Tom in the garden again. He often returned from a walk like that, by the side door, not coming into the house at once, strolling about, dead-heading if the season called for that. She washed the parsley he'd earlier picked for her, and chopped it finely, ready for the carrots, the two bright colours of the tricolour – she'd never noticed that until Tom said one suppertime. He'd taken her away from the window and she'd whispered, 'Poor Joe Paddy!' because she was confused, and he said no, it wasn't Joe Paddy who'd been shot. She asked him then and he said: because he had to, because she had to know. He hadn't let her look.

'Would you like a sherry?' Tom was suddenly there, as earlier he'd been when he'd told her he'd finished his book.

'Sherry would be nice,' she said.

Anglesea Street, she thought, a little flat in Anglesea Street, plumb in the middle of Dublin. She'd always been attracted by that narrow street, not far from Tom's office, not far from Jury's Hotel, where sometimes they met for a cup of coffee in his lunchtime. They'd still do that, of course, and as often as she was welcome she'd visit Rathfarnham – at weekends, Saturday lunch, whatever was convenient. She could say so now; it was a time to do so, while they drank their sherry.

'There was an old man I don't remember seeing before,' Tom said. 'By the bridge.'

'He's come to live with the Mulcahys. Her father.'

'Ah.'

Children would run about the garden again. There would be their laughter, and family birthdays. She would bring her presents, and with the years Tom would slip into their father's role and be like him too, easygoing, with jokes to tell. The children would tell her things, have secrets with her, as sometimes children did with an aunt.

She heard the clink of the decanter's stopper, the sherry poured, and then Tom brought the two glasses from the dining-room. It was extraordinary that the officer who came had wept in front of them. He had alarmed them, weeping so suddenly, so unnaturally, the brick-hued flesh of his heavy face crumpling into dismay and grief. 'The waste of it,' he mumbled. 'The waste of it.' The soldier who had gone berserk in mistaking Joe Paddy for someone else had suffered shell-shock. His officer – in charge of him, responsible, he wretchedly insisted – could hardly explain, so clogged with emotion his voice was. He did not know, for it did not concern him, that Joe Paddy's connection with the house he'd sought refuge in when he was pursued through the streets was as tenuous as the unbalanced soldier's was with Joe Paddy: once every two months or so Joe Paddy came to clean its windows. Madness and death: that's how it was in war, this big, ruddy officer had said. As long as he lived, he made a kind of promise, he would not be able to forget what had happened in a suburban garden.

'We're nearly ready,' Philippa said in the kitchen, but her brother made her pause for a moment to sip her sherry while he mashed the potatoes and sprinkled in the chopped-up chives.

'Tom,' she said and found it difficult to continue, and he smiled at her as if he perfectly divined her thoughts. He even slightly shook his head, although she was not entirely sure about that and perhaps he didn't. Intent upon his task again, he turned away and she did not continue.

She imagined, in a small low-ceilinged sitting-room a coal fire spluttering a bit, a single blue flame among insipid spurts of orange. People didn't live much in Anglesea Street, it wasn't that kind of street, but that would suit her – the sound of handcarts down below, voices faintly calling out.

'Thank you,' she said, finishing her sherry when she saw that Tom had finished his. She rinsed the glasses. Thirty-four years, she calculated; she would be seventy-three when the same time had passed again, Tom would be seventy-six. 1984 it would be, sixteen years from the century's end, as 1916 had been from the beginning.

He helped her carry the dishes into the dining-room and then he poured the wine. It did not seem an error now, that he had bought it. The wine would make it easier to say, the sherry and the wine together.

'There's talk of a new road,' he said. 'Out near Marley.'

'I hadn't heard that.'

'Oh, some time well into the future they're talking of.'

'Maybe it won't happen.'

Once on this Sunday he had predicted more war and more war had come; he had predicted Ireland's wise neutrality and had been right. He would hate a big new road out there. He hated the motorcycles that roared up Tibradden, that crashed through fern and undergrowth and little woods, that muddied the streams. One day the crawl of lorries would take the freshness from the air.

'Tom,' she said again. She was wondering, she began, and paused, a natural pause it seemed. *13 Anglesea St.*, it said on an envelope, and they crossed College Green from Trinity, and then she heard their footsteps on the stairs. She made them coffee because coffee was what they liked, and cut the Bewley's cake, ready for them. Why thirteen? she wondered, and wondered then if even now there was an empty flat there, if some premonition had winkled that out for her. Long legs her nephew had, like his father; her niece was beautiful already.

'This summer?' Tom said. 'Port-na-Blagh, d'you think?'
He had been patient, not saying anything. A kindness that
was, and his smile was a kindness too. 'Port-na-Blagh?' he
said again.

She nodded, making herself because he had been kind.
She talked about the summer because he wanted to. Three
weeks away from Dublin and Rathfarnham, the sands at
Port-na-Blagh unchanged, the white farmhouse, the hens
that pecked about its yard. She loved it too, as much as he
did, when they locked up and went away to Donegal. Even
when it rained and her summer dresses remained unpacked,
when they gazed from the windows at their ruined days or
crunched over pebbles that never dried. They always brought
more books than they could read, denuding the shelves of
the Argosy Lending Library, owing a bit on them when they
returned.

'Or somewhere else, d'you think?' he said.

They'd gone to Glandore once, another year to Ross-
league, but Port-na-Blagh they still liked best. 'I wonder what
became of those widowed brothers,' Tom said, and she
knew at once whom he meant: two Guinness clerks who'd
been widowed in the same year, who hardly spoke in the
boarding-house dining-room; on Achill that was. And the
school inspector who spoke in Irish came for a few nights to
Glandore.

'July again?' she said.

'I'm afraid so.'

'It's often fine enough.'

He nodded, and she could tell he was longing for a cigarette. But it wasn't his way to smoke during a meal; she'd never seen him doing that.

'Yes, of course it is,' he said.

*

He saw, again, the effort in her eyes, and sensed her saying to herself that it would not be difficult, that he would listen, that the words were simple. Once, a while ago, maybe as long ago as fifteen years, she had said it; and again, more recently, had come closer to saying it than she had tonight.

'Low Sunday it is called, you know,' he said.

'Yes, I did know.'

He poured the last of the wine in the silence that had gathered. Once she had wept when he was not there; he knew because her smile was different when he returned, the marks of tears powdered over. Now, it was easier. Only Low Sunday held them in its thrall, her head pressed into the wool of his jersey, his voice not letting her look. Pity for his romantic ghosts still kept the moment at bay; she had her fantasy of the future. Fragments of intuition were their conversation, real beneath the unreal words. No one else would understand: tomorrow, she would once more know that.

They gathered the dishes and the plates from the table and took them to the kitchen. He washed up, as he always did at weekends. She put things away. The tired dog lay sleeping in his kennel. The downstairs lights were one by one extinguished.

Low Sunday, 1950

The past receded a little with the day; time yet unspent was left to happen as fearfully as it would. Night settled, there was no sound. Tranquil 1950 was again a haven in Ireland's dark.

Le Visiteur

Once a year, when summer was waning, Guy went to the island. And once a year, as his visit drew to a close, he took Monsieur and Madame Buissonnet out to dinner at the hotel. He had not always done so, for he had first received the Buissonnets' invitation to visit them when he was seven. He was thirty-two now, no longer placed by his mother in the care of the ferryman for the journey from Port Vevey and by Madame Buissonnet for the journey back. For thirteen years there had been the tradition of dinner at the hotel, the drive from the farm in the onion truck, Madame Buissonnet in her grey and black, Monsieur Buissonnet teasingly not taking off his boatman's cap until they were almost in the restaurant, then stuffing it into his pocket. *Loup de mer*: always the same for both of them, and as often as not for Guy also. *Soupe de langoustines* to start with.

'Well, now,' Madame Buissonnet said, as she always did when the order had been given, the Macon Fuissé tasted. 'Well, now?' she repeated, for dinner at the hotel was the occasion for such revelations as had not yet been divulged during Guy's stay.

'Gérard married,' he said. 'Jean-Claude has gone to Africa.'

'*Africa?*'

'Maybe for ever. I miss him.'

Monsieur Buissonnet listened less intently than his wife did, his eye roving about the restaurant, lingering occasionally on a beautiful face. Sometimes he softly sighed. 'Your mother?' he had enquired in a private moment on the first afternoon of Guy's visit, as every year he did. As far as Madame Buissonnet was concerned, Guy's mother might not have existed.

'And you are promoted a step higher, Guy?' she asked now.

'It is once in three years, that.'

'Ah, yes.'

'My dear.' Monsieur Buissonnet placed a hand over one of his wife's, his endearment gently reassuring her that it didn't matter if she had forgotten promotion did not come every single year.

'How agreeable it is here,' she murmured, turning her palm upward for a moment and smiling a smile she reserved for such moments. Guy felt not included in this occasion of communication between the couple, even though he was responsible for their presence here. A silence fell, then Monsieur Buissonnet said:

'It was nothing once, this place.'

'It has made a *milliard* since,' his wife reminded him. Or two, he agreed. A man who knew how to make money was Perdreau. Yet every dish you ate in his restaurant was worth its francs.

White-haired, a shock still falling over his forehead, Monsieur Buissonnet possessed the remnants of handsome features, as his wife did of beauty. Nothing would be regained by either of them; the disturbances of time and sun were there for ever. Yet the toll was softened: the whiteness of their hair, and its abundance, was an attraction in old age; that he was leaner than he had ever been brought out in Monsieur Buissonnet qualities of distinction that had not been evident before; his wife's fragility complemented the slenderness she had never lost.

'And now what else?' she enquired when *les amuse-gueules* were finished.

Guy talked about Club 14 because he could think of nothing else. It was odd, it always seemed to him, what was said and what was not; and not just here, not only by the Buissonnets. His mother had never asked a single thing about the island, or even mentioned the Buissonnets except, in his childhood, to say when September was half over that it was time for him to visit them again. Once he had tried to tell her of the acre or two Monsieur Buissonnet and his labourers had reclaimed for cultivation during the year that had passed, how *oliviers* or vines had been planted where only scrub had grown before, how a few more metres had been marked out for irrigation. His mother had never displayed an interest. 'Oh, it is because they have no children of their own,' she'd said when he asked why it was that the Buissonnets invited him. 'It is so sometimes.'

Not that Guy objected to being invited. He was as fond of the farm and the island as he was of the Buissonnets themselves. He delighted in the dry, parched earth, the *crêtes*, the unsafe cliffs. Dust coated the vegetation, the giant cacti, the purple or scarlet ipomoea with which the villagers decorated their walls, the leaves of brambles and oleander. It invaded cypresses and heather and the rock roses that Guy had never seen in flower. Only the huge stones and well-washed pebbles of the little bays escaped its grey deposit. Only the eucalyptus trees and the plane trees rose above it.

The accompaniments of the *soupe de langoustines* came, the waiter unfamiliar, new this season as the waiters often were. He placed the dishes he brought where they might easily be reached by all three diners, then ladled out the soup. He poured more Macon Fuissé.

'What style!' Madame Buissonnet whispered when he had passed on to another table, and then, 'How good you are to take us here again, Guy!'

'It's nothing.'

'Oh, but yes, it is, my dear.'

The restaurant of the hotel had views over a valley to a lush growth of trees, unusual on the island. A carpet of grass, broken by oleander beds, formed the valley's base, far below the level of the restaurant itself. This was shadowy now in the September twilight, the colour drained from its daytime's splendour. The lengths of blue and white awning that earlier had protected the lunchtime diners from the sun had been rolled in, the sliding glass panels closed against mosquitoes. Thirty tables, a stiff white tablecloth on each, were widely separated in the airy, circular space, a couple of them unoccupied tonight. Monsieur Perdreau, the hotel's proprietor for as long as Guy and the Buissonnets had been dining in its restaurant, was making his evening tour, pausing at each table to introduce himself or to ensure that everything was in order.

The Buissonnets knew him well, and by now so did Guy. He stayed a while, receiving compliments, bowing his gratitude, giving some details of his season, which had, this year, been particularly good, even if the restaurant was not quite full tonight. The hotel itself was, he explained: it was just that at the moment there were fewer yachts moored at the harbour.

'You are getting to be my oldest client, Guy,' he said, shaking hands before he went away.

It was then that Guy noticed that the girl two tables away had been joined by a companion. She was in white, fair-haired, slight; the man was bulky, in a bright blue suit. Guy had noticed the girl earlier and had thought it singular that being on her own she should want to occupy so prominent a table.

'Splendid!' Monsieur Buissonnet exclaimed when the waiter returned with the soup tureen.

*

The evening advanced, pleasurably and easily, as in previous Septembers so many others had. The *loup de mer* was as good as ever; glasses of Margaux accompanied the cheese. Madame Buissonnet's disappointment that Guy had been unable to report a new relationship in his life was kept in check. She asked about Colette, who for a time had been Guy's fiancée, and bravely smiled when she heard that Colette had become engaged to André Délespaul. Monsieur Buissonnet talked about the olive harvest, the coldest November he could remember on the island because of the bitter wind, how it had suddenly got up and remained for weeks, a mistral out of season. But none the less the harvest had been a good one.

Vanilla ice-cream came, a mango *coulis*. The little *boules* were so elegantly arranged on the green, yellow-rimmed plates that Madame Buissonnet said it was a pity to disturb them. The man in the blue suit had again left his companion on her own. She sat very still, eating nothing now. Coffee was brought to her but she did not pour it out. A cup and saucer were placed for her companion, beside his crumpled napkin.

'They are a pest sometimes,' Monsieur Buissonnet said, an observation he now and again made about the tourists who came to the island, 'even if they bring a bit of life.'

The tourists hired bicycles at the harbour or in the village and rode about the sandy tracks. They came for the day or lodged in one of the small village hotels if not in Monsieur Perdreau's rather grander one. The only vehicles that were permitted on the island were the farm trucks, the tractors, the delivery vans, and the minibus that delivered and collected guests. Cigarettes were forbidden in wooded areas because of the risk of fire.

'Oh, we enjoy the tourists,' Madame Buissonnet commented. 'Of course we do.'

One by one, the tables were deserted. When the waiter whom Madame Buissonnet considered stylish brought chocolates and coffee, only a few were still occupied – the one at which the girl sat alone, a corner one at which Italian was spoken, a third at which a couple now stood up. The man in the blue suit returned, his progress unsteady and laboured, an apologetic smile thrown about, as if he were unaware that the chairs he circumvented were empty. He sat down noisily and at once stood up again, seeming to seek the attention of a waiter. When one approached he waved him away but, still on his feet, filled his glass and spilt it as he sat down. The girl poured coffee. She did not speak.

'*È oritologo,*' someone said at the Italian table, a woman's voice carrying across the restaurant. '*Scrive libri sugli uccelli.*'

The man in the blue suit stood up and again looked around him. He pulled at the knot of his tie, loosening it. He groped beneath it for the buttons of his shirt. His companion stared at the tablecloth. Was she weeping? Guy wondered. Something about her bent head suggested that she might be.

There was a glisten of sweat on the man's forehead and his cheeks. He raised his glass in the direction of the Italians, smiling at them foolishly. One of them – a man in a suede jacket – bowed stiffly.

The waiters stood back, perfectly discreet. Amused at first by the scene, Madame Buissonnet now glanced away from what was happening. They should be going, she said.

'*Mi dà i brividi,*' one of the Italians exclaimed quite loudly, and they all got up, the women gathering handbags and shawls, one of the men lighting a fresh cigarette.

Watching them go, Guy realized that all evening he had been stealing glances at the girl who shared the drunk man's table. Especially when she was alone he had kept glancing at her, unable to prevent himself. She was very thin. He had never seen a girl as thin. All the time he had talked about Gérard and Jean-Claude, and André Délespaul and Colette, all the time he had listened to the details of the olive harvest, while he'd shaken Monsieur Perdreau's hand and laughed at his joke, he had imagined being with her in the little bay where he swam and at Le Nautic or the Café Vert in the village. He had looked for a wedding ring, and there it was.

The drunk man laughed. He waved at the Italians, his laughter louder, as if he and they shared some moment of comedy. The one who'd just lit a cigarette waved back.

'Hi!' the drunk man called after them, and lurched across the restaurant, knocking into the chairs and tables, apologizing to people who weren't there. He stopped suddenly, as if his energy had failed him. He was confused. He frowned, shaking his head.

It wasn't a real smile when the girl smiled at Guy; it was too joyless for that, with a kind of pleading in it. She smiled because all evening she had been aware he'd been unable to take his eyes off her. Had she really once married this man? Guy wondered. Could they really be husband and wife?

'Thank you, Guy,' Madame Buissonnet said, as she always did when the evening ended. The bill came swiftly when he gestured for it. He signed the *carte bancaire*.

'Yes,' Monsieur Buissonnet said. 'Thank you.'

It was then that the man fell down. He fell on to an unlaid table and slithered sideways to the ground. Waiters came to help him up, but he managed to scramble to his feet by himself. His wife didn't look. Guy was certain now she was his wife.

'Hi!' the man shouted at the Buissonnets. 'Hi!'

He was laughing again and he shouted something else but Guy couldn't understand what it was because the man spoke in either English or German; it was difficult to distinguish which because his voice was slurred. He clattered down, into the chair he'd been sitting on before. He spread his arms out on the tablecloth and sank his head into them. The girl said something, but he didn't move.

Guy didn't let his anger show. He was good at that; he always had been. It could happen like this that you fell in love, that there was some moment you didn't notice at the time and afterwards couldn't find when you thought back. It didn't matter because you knew it was there, because you knew that this had happened.

'I talked to those people on my walk today.' It seemed hardly a lie, just something it was necessary to say. Anything would have done.

Madame Buissonnet displayed no surprise, accepting Guy's claim without a knowing smile. A man of the world in such matters, Monsieur Buissonnet said the key to the farmhouse would be where it always was when it was left outside: in the dovecot. 'Madame must have her beauty sleep,' he added, tucking his wife's arm into his.

*

'It is no trouble.'

Again Guy imagined being with her in the little bay, and

telling her in Le Nautic or the Café Vert why he was on the island, explaining about the Buissonnets, explaining why it was that he had been in the restaurant when first they saw one another, how he had told the Buissonnets a lie, how they had guessed it was a lie, and how that didn't matter.

'Madame,' a waiter murmured, offering help, repeating what Guy had said – that it was no trouble – pretending that nothing much had happened.

The man in the blue suit was awake and on his feet, squeezing his eyes closed, as if to clear what was faulty in his vision, blinking them open again. Guy and the waiter helped him across the restaurant, across the foyer to the lift. The girl who had been humiliated whispered her gratitude, seeming not to have the confidence to raise her voice. She looked even thinner, even frailer, when she was on her feet.

On Sunday, on the last of the evening ferries, Guy would leave the island, his visit over. Even sooner she might go herself, first thing in the morning, hurrying off with her companion because of the shame they shared. In the lift there was no embarrassment when they touched, her shoulder pressed on Guy's because the lift was small. He felt panic spreading, affecting his heartbeat, a dryness in his mouth. Yet how could she go so swiftly when she had pleaded so? Where had the pleading come from if not from their being aware of one another? Alone at her table when her boorish husband left her to fend for herself, she had been disturbed by a stranger's gaze and had not rejected it. Why had she not unless she'd known as certainly as he? Even before they heard one another's voices, there had been that certainty of knowing. All intuition, all just a feeling across a distance, and yet more than they had ever known before.

'*Voilà!*' the waiter murmured, producing the key of the couple's room from one of the man's pockets. A moment before there had been consternation when it could not be found.

Love was conversation: Gérard had said that, and Guy had never understood until tonight. They would sit on the rocks and their conversation would spread itself around them, their two lives tangling, as in a different way they had already begun to. Club 14, Gérard, Jean-Claude, Jean-Pierre, Colette, Michelle, Dominique, Adrien, the walk from the rue Marceau to the Café de la Paix after a badminton game, his mother, and all the rest of what there was: tomorrow and Saturday were not enough. Well, of course they did not have to be.

She gave the waiter a hundred-franc note when the man had been dumped on the bed. The waiter put the room key on the writing-table. When he went he did not seem surprised that Guy did not go also, perhaps sensing something of what had come about. Only once in a whole lifetime, Guy thought, fate offered two people this. 'How much a visitor you are!' Michelle said once, and truth to tell he had always felt so, not quite belonging in the group, not even with his mother. And with the Buissonnets, of course, he was a visitor too. All that would come into the conversation; everything would in the end.

'Thank you,' she said, speaking in English, and then in French in case he had not understood. But he could manage a little English, and wondered if these were Americans or English people. On the bed the man was snoring.

'Please,' she said, opening the minibar and gesturing toward its array of little bottles. 'Please have something.'

He wanted to say she mustn't feel embarrassed. He wanted to reassure her absolutely, to say that what had occurred downstairs was of no possible consequence. He wanted to talk of all the other matters immediately, to tell her that years ago he had guessed that Monsieur Buissonnet was his father, that he was certain he owed his position in the Crédit Lyonnais to Monsieur Buissonnet's influence. He wanted to tell her that nothing was ever said – not a word – by Madame Buissonnet about his mother, or by his mother about Madame Buissonnet, that he had long ago guessed his mother had been a woman in Monsieur Buissonnet's life before his marriage. It would have been before his marriage; it was not Monsieur Buissonnet's style to be unfaithful.

'Oh, then, a cognac,' he said.

It was not ever said that the farm would one day be his. That was why Monsieur Buissonnet talked so often and so much about it, why Madame Buissonnet asked if this was right, or that, when she chose the colours for a room she wanted to have repainted.

Guy took the glass that was held out to him and for a second his fingers brushed the fingers of the girl he had fallen in love with. He had not known until tonight that it was something you could tell in minutes, even seconds, when you first loved somebody.

'You have been kind,' she said. She sat in a low armchair

beside the minibar and Guy sat by the writing-table. She flattened the skirt of her white dress over her knees. So much about her was like a child, he thought: her hands as they passed over the white material, the outline of her knees, her feet in high-heeled shoes. Her fair hair fell tidily, framing an image of features in which he believed he could still detect the lingering of the hurt she'd suffered. Her eyes were blue, as pale as the sky there'd been that day.

'Are you American?' he asked, carefully speaking English, translating the question from the French.

'Yes, American.'

It was awkward, the man being there, even though he was asleep. His mood might not be pleasant if he woke up, yet it did not seem to matter; it was only awkward. Guy said:

'I have only been in the restaurant of the hotel before. Not in a room.'

'You are not staying here?'

'No, no.'

She went to the bed and pushed the man on to his side, exerting herself to do so. The snoring ceased.

'I come every year to the island,' Guy said. 'The Buissonnets have a farm.'

'The people you were with?'

'Yes.'

'I have never been here before.'

'People find it tranquil.'

'Yes, it's that.'

When she sat down again the gaze they held one another in was as bold as for each of them it had been downstairs, as open and as confident. Guy hadn't realized then that this confidence had been there, and the openness. He wondered if – until she smiled – he had assumed that in the unobtrusive lighting of the restaurant she had failed to notice his obsessive interest. He couldn't remember what he had assumed and it didn't seem to be important. He wondered what she was thinking.

'We came by chance here,' she said. 'To the island.'

'Yes.'

'Please don't get up and go.'

He shook his head. She smiled and he smiled back. He would show her everything on the island, and when the moment for it came he would tell her that he loved her. He would tell her that never before had he loved a girl like this, had only been attracted in the more ordinary way. That could be because he was what Michelle had called a visitor, always a little on his own. It could have to do with the circumstances of his birth, so little being said, nothing whatso-ever really. Who can tell? Guy wondered. Who can tell what makes a person what he is?

'May I ask your name?'

'It's Guy.'

She didn't give hers. Guy was nice, she said, especially as it was said in France. It suited him, the French way of saying it.

'Some more?' she offered.

He had hardly drunk a drop. He shook his head. She reached out to close the door of the minibar, shutting away the light that through its array of bottles had been falling on the thin calves of her legs. They would have a marriage like the Buissonnets'; in the farmhouse it would be like that. Slowly she reached down and took her shoes off.

*

The jaw of the man on the bed had fallen open. An arm hung down, fingers trailing the carpet quite close to where they were.

'Guy,' she whispered, her white dress in a bundle on the floor, one of her shoes on its side. 'My dear,' she whispered.

There was an urgency in her resistance to his drawing back from the act that was pressed upon him. There were no whispers now, and no caresses. Instinctively Guy knew there was no pleasure for her. She laughed when it was over, a soundless laugh, different from her husband's yet it echoed that.

The room was stifling, the air gone stale, infected by the rank breath of the man who slept. Naked, she stood above him, looking down at his slumbering features, at the stubble that was beginning on his chin and neck, a dribble running from a corner of his mouth. She touched his shoulder, and for an instant his eyes opened. She said nothing, and he slept again. For all this – for what had happened, for what was happening still – she had returned a stranger's gaze. Destruction was present in the room; Guy was aware of that.

She turned away, from the bed where her husband lay, from Guy. The drink she'd poured herself had not been touched. Guy watched her cross the room and close a door behind her. He heard the running of her bath.

He dressed, separating his clothes from hers. He might go to her, now that these minutes had elapsed. Tomorrow, he might say. In the Café Vert at half past ten, ten if it suited better. He would show her the island, he would show her the farm; she would tell him about herself. It could not be forgotten, what had happened, there could be no pretence; yet when they talked, when their conversation began, what had happened would not belong in it.

He laid her dress, with her underclothes, on a chair, arranged her shoes one beside the other on the floor. He drank the cognac, leaving none of it, wanting it because she'd poured it for him. Then he tapped on the door she'd closed.

Her voice came at once, harsh and loud, as it had not been before.

'I'm having a bath. You'll have to wait.'

She spoke in English. Guy understood the first sentence, but had to think about the second, and in thinking realized that it was the sleeping man who was addressed, that he himself should already have gone away. About to reply, to correct this misunderstanding, he hesitated.

'Look about you while you're waiting.' Mockery was added to the other qualities that had come into her voice. 'Why not do that?'

She would have liked it better had he woken up properly when she touched his shoulder; it was second best, her clothes thrown about, the two glasses where they'd been left. It was second best but even so it was enough. And the room's impressions of what had taken place still hung about it.

Guy's footsteps were soundless on the carpet as he moved

away. He glanced as he passed the bed at the man in the bright blue suit, some spillage of food whitening a lapel, cheeks and forehead florid. He wondered what his name was, hers too, before he left the room.

*

The night air was cold, already the air of autumn. Slowly progressing on the dusty track, Guy wondered what the Buissonnets had said to one another. They might mention the incident in the morning, or might have decided that they should not.

The sea lapped softly over the pebbles of the bay where he swam. He sat down among the rocks, wondering if he would ever tell anyone, and if he did how exactly he would put it. It was how they lived, he might say; it was how they belonged to one another, not that he understood. In the cold bright moonlight he felt his solitude a comfort.

The Virgin's Gift

A gentle autumn had slipped away, sunny to the end, the last of the butterflies still there in December, dozing in the crevices of the rocks. The lingering petals of the rock flowers had months before faded and fallen from their stems; the heather was in bloom, the yellow of the gorse had quietened. It was a miracle, Michael often thought, a summer marvel that the butterflies came to his place at all.

Feeling that he had walked all Ireland – an expression used often in the very distant past that was his time – Michael had arrived at Ireland's most ragged edge. He knew well that there was land to the north, and to the west and east, which he had not travelled, that no man could walk all Ireland's riverbanks and tracks, its peaks and plains, through every spinney, along every cliff, through every gorge. But the exaggeration of the expression offered something in the way of sense; his journey, for him, had been what the words implied. Such entanglements of truth and falsity – and of good and evil, God and the devil – Michael dwelt upon in the hermitage he had created, while the seasons changed and the days of his life were one by one extinguished.

The seasons announced themselves, but for the days he kept a calendar – as by rule they had at the abbey – his existence shaped by feast days and fasting days, by days of penance and of rest. Among the rocks of his island, time was neither enemy nor friend, its passing no more than an element that belonged with the sea and the shores, the garden of vegetables he had cultivated, the habitation he had made, the gulls, the solitude. He sensed the character of each one of the seven days and kept alive the different feeling that each inspired, knowing when he awoke which one it was.

When the fourth day in December came it was St Peter Chrysologus's. There was more dark than light now, and soon rain and wind would take possession of the craggy landscape. At first, in winter, he had lost his way in the mists that came at this time too, when all that was familiar to him became distorted; now, he knew better than to venture far. In December each day that was not damp, each bitter morning, each starry night, was as welcome as the summer flowers and butterflies.

When he was eighteen Michael's vocation had been revealed to him, an instruction coming in a dream that he should leave the farm and offer himself at the abbey. He hardly knew about the abbey then, having heard it mentioned only once or twice in conversation, and was hazy as to its purpose or its nature. 'Oh, you'd never want to,' Fódla said when he told her, for ever since they'd first embraced he had told her everything. 'You'd go there when you're old,' she hopefully conjectured, but her dark eyes were sad already, a finger twisting a loop of hair, the way she did when she was unhappy. 'A dream's no more'n a dream,' she whispered in useless protestation when he repeated how the Virgin had appeared, bearing God's message.

Cutting new sods for his roof on the morning of St Peter Chrysologus's day, Michael remembered Fódla's tears. They had played together since they were infants – on the earthen floor of the outside house where the feed was boiled, on the dug-out turf bogs while the donkeys patiently waited to have their panniers filled, on the stubble of the cornfield where her father and his worked together to raise the stooks, their mothers too, her brothers when they were old enough. 'I have to,' he said when Fódla wept, and near to where they walked a bird warbled for a moment, as if to mock her sorrow. Her hand slipped out of his, their friendship over. Her life, too, she said.

'God has spoken for you.' His father took a different view that same evening. 'And by that He has honoured you. Do not have doubt, Michael.'

He did not have doubt, only concern that God's honouring of him would one day mean the farm's decline: he was an only child.

'He will provide,' his father reassured, sturdy and confident, in the prime of his life. 'He surely will.'

Michael carried from the other side of his island the first sods of scrappy grass he had cut. Back and forth he went all morning, until he had a stack beside his shelter. Then he lifted the sods into place, twelve rows of six on the two slight inclines of the roof, beating them together with the long, flat stone he kept for the purpose. Three sides of his shelter were constructed as he had long ago learned to build a field wall, the stones set at an angle. The fourth was a natural hollow in the rock-face, and the frame on which he laid the sods was of branches lashed together, door and door-frame made similarly.

He had soothed with dock leaves Fódla's arms when they were stung. When she was frightened of the orchard geese he had taken her from them and soon after that she was frightened of nothing. She would be married now, children and grandchildren born to her, the friendship of so far back forgotten: he accepted that. His mother would be eighty years old, his father older still. Or they would not be there at all, which was more likely.

Michael saved the salt of the sea, and in summer preserved with it the fish he caught. The grain he had first cultivated from the seed he brought from the abbey continued year by year. There were the hurtleberries, the patch of nettles he had encouraged and extended, the mossy seaweed that ripened in the sun, the spring that never failed, the herbs he'd grown from roots brought from the abbey also. 'Find solitude,' the Virgin had instructed the second time, after he had been seventeen years at the abbey, and again it seemed like punishment, as it had on the morning of Fódla's tears.

When it was twilight and the task of repairing his roof was complete, Michael climbed to the highest crag of the island to look across at the mainland cliffs he had so long ago waded away from, with all he had brought with him held above his head. From the sky he predicted tomorrow's weather; it would still be fine. Skimpy tails of cloud did not disturb the trail of amber left behind after the sun had slipped away. The sea was placid as a lake.

Often on evenings as tranquil as this Michael imagined he could hear the Angelus bell at the abbey, although he knew that was impossible. In his time there he had come to love the discipline and the order, the simplicity of the few pleasures there had been, the companionship. The dawn processing from the cloisters to the high cross in the pasture, the evening lamps lit, the chanting of the psalter, the murmur of the Mass – all that, even now, he missed. Brother Luchan knew the saints and told their stories: how St Mellitus refused to give the Blessed Sacrament to the king's sons, how wolves and bears were obedient to St Marcian, how St Simeon scourged himself on pillars. In their cells Cronan and Murtagh illuminated the Scriptures, compounding inks and cutting pens. Ioin had a lazy eye, Bernard was as tubby as a barrel, Fintan fresh-cheeked and happy. Diarmaid was the tallest, Conor the best at conversation, Tomás the most forgetful, Cathal the practical one. 'Never lose your piece of glass,' Cathal warned in his farewell. 'Never be without the means of fire.'

Did they see him, as he could still see them – his tattered habit, his tonsure gone, beard trimmed as well as he could manage, bare feet? Did they imagine the cross scratched on the stone above the ledge that was his bed? Did they hear in their mind's ear the waves, and the wailing of the gulls while he hauled over the rocks the seaweed to his garden plot? Did they guess he still visited in his thoughts the little pond beyond the coppice, and watched the decorating of a verse, the play of creatures arrested by Cronan's pen, fish and birds, snakes coiled about a letter's stem?

It was as Murtagh had represented her that the Virgin
came to him the second time, not as she had been before,
which was in a likeness that was almost his mother's. He had
not understood, that second time, why there should again be
disruption in his life. He understood now. At the abbey he
had learned piety, had practised patience, been humbled by
his companions' talents, strengthened by their friendship.
But in his solitude he was closer to God.

Still standing on the crag that rose above the others, he
knew that with a certainty that came freshly to him in the
evening of every day. During all his time here he had not seen
another person, had spoken only to God and to himself, to
animals and birds and the butterflies that so strangely arrived,
occasionally to an insect. The figments that congregated in his
imagination did not create an alien mood; nostalgia was always
checked. This evening, as he prepared his food and ate it, it
pleased him that he had cut the roof sods and settled them
into place while it was fine. That was a satisfaction, and he
took it with him when he lay down to rest.

*

Colour came from nowhere, brightening to a vividness.
There was a fluttering of wings closing after flight, scarlet
birds of paradise, yellow-breasted, green. Archways receded
into landscape; faint brown and pink were washed through
the marble tracery of a floor. Rays of sunlight were like
arrows in the sky.

The Virgin's dress was two shades of blue, her lacy halo
hardly there. This time her features were not reminiscent of

what Michael's mother's once had been, nor of a gospel illumination: there was such beauty as Michael had never before beheld in a human face or anywhere in nature – not in the rock flowers or the heather, not in the delicacy of the seashore shells. Pale, slender hands were raised in a gesture of affection.

'Michael,' the Virgin said and there was a stillness until, unkempt and ragged, he stood before her, until he said:

'I am content here.'

'Because you have come to love your solitude, Michael.'

'Yes.'

'In this month of the year you must leave it.'

'I was content on my father's farm. I was content at the abbey. This is my place now.'

Through denial and deprivation he had been led to peace, a destination had been reached. These words were not spoken but were there, a thought passing through the conversation.

'I have come to you the last time now,' the Virgin said.

She did not smile and yet was not severe in the serenity that seemed to spread about her. Delicately, the fingers of her hands touched and parted, and then were raised in blessing.

'I cannot understand,' Michael said, struggling to find other words and remaining silent when he could not. Then it was dark again, until he woke at dawn.

*

It was a Thursday. Michael sensed that in nervous irritation. The day of the week was irrelevant when, this morning, there was so much else. 'Blessed among women,' he beseeched. 'Our Lady of grace, hear me.'

He begged that his melancholy might be lifted, that the confusion which had come in the night might be lightened with revelation. These were the days of the year when his spirits were most joyful, when each hour that passed brought closer the celebration of the Saviour's birth. Why had this honouring of a season been so brutally upset?

'Blessed among women,' Michael murmured again, but when he rose from his knees he was still alone.

The greyness of early morning made his island greyer than it often was, and the images of the dream – brightly lingering – made it greyer still. 'A dream's no more'n a dream,' Fódla's young voice echoed from the faraway past, and Michael saw his own head shaking a denial. Though feeling punished after the previous occasions of the Virgin's presence, he had not experienced the unease of irritation. He had not, in all his life, experienced it often. At the abbey there had been the dragging walk of Brother Andrew, his sandals flapping, a slow, repetitive sound that made you close your eyes and silently urge him to hurry. Every time Brother Justus stood up from the refectory table he shook the crumbs from the lap of his habit, scattering them so that the floor would have to be swept again. There was old Nessan's cough.

This morning, though, Michael's distress was bleaker than any mood engendered by such pinpricks of annoyance. The prospect of moving out of his solitude was fearful. This was his place and he had made it so. In his fifty-ninth year, it would enfeeble him to travel purposelessly. He would not bear a journey with the fortitude he had possessed in his boyhood and in his middle age. If he was being called to his death, why might he not die here, among his stones, close to his heather and his gorse, close to his little garden of lettuces and roots?

Slowly, when a little more time had passed, he made his way to the different shores of the island. He stood in the mouth of the cave where he had lived before he built his shelter. Then – twenty-one years ago – he had thought he would not survive. He had failed when he tried to trap the fish, had not yet developed a taste for the sloes that were the nourishment his fastness offered. He had tried to attract bees, but no bees came. He had hoped a bramble might yield blackberries, but it was not the kind to do so. Before he found the spring he drank from a pool in the bog.

From the cave he could see the stunted oak trees of the island's headland, bent back to the ground, and he remembered how at first they had seemed sinister, the wind that shaped them hostile. But this morning they were friendly and the breeze that blew in from the sea was so slight it still did not disturb the water's surface. The waves lapped softly on the shingle. For years the gulls had not feared him and they alighted near him now, strutting a little on the rocks and then becoming still.

'I am content here,' Michael said aloud, saying it again because it was the truth. Head bent in shame, shoulders hunched beneath the habit that no longer offered much warmth or protection, eyes closed and seeing nothing, Michael struggled with his anger. Had his obedience not been enough? Had he been vain, or proud? Should he not have taken even one egg from the gulls' nests?

No answer came, none spoken, none felt, and he was surly when he sought forgiveness for questions that were presumptuous.

*

He crossed to the cliffs when the tide was low enough, wading through the icy water that soaked him up to his breast. He took his habit off and shivered as he squeezed the sea out of it, laying it on a rock to catch the sun. He beat at his body with his arms and clenched his fingers into his palms to restore the circulation.

He waited an hour, then dressed again, all he put on still damp. He felt himself watched by the gulls, and wondered if they sensed that something was different about the place he'd shared with them. He climbed the cliff-face, finding footholds easily, hauling himself up by grasping the spiky rock. At the top there was a ridge of bitten grass and then the gorse began, and became so dense he thought at first he would not be able to make a way through it. The thorns tore at his legs and feet, drawing blood, until he came upon a clearing where the vegetation had failed. It narrowed, then snaked on ahead of him, like a track.

He walked until it was dark, stopping only to pick crab-apples and to drink from a stream. He lay down to rest on a growth of ferns, placing over him for warmth those he had rooted up. He slept easily and deeply, although he had thought he would not.

The next morning he passed a tower that was deserted, with nothing left of its one-time habitation. He passed a dwelling outside which a jennet was tethered. In a field a young man and woman were weeding a winter crop. They told him where he was, but he had never heard of the neighbourhood they mentioned, nor of a town two hours further on. He asked for water and they gave him milk, the first he had tasted since he left the abbey. They gave him bread and black pudding that had a herb in it, marjoram, they said. They guessed he was a *seanchaí* but he said no, not adding that the only story he had to tell was his own, wondering how they would respond if he revealed that Our Lady had three times appeared to him in a dream.

'Are you walking all Ireland?' the young man asked, making conversation with that familiar expression. Their hoes laid down, the two sat with him on a verge of grass while he ate and drank.

'I have walked it before,' he replied. 'In the way you mean.'

'Not many pass us here.'

They spoke between themselves, establishing when last there had been a visitor on the way that was close to them. They had the field and the jennet, they said when he asked. It wouldn't be long before an infant was born to them.

'You are prosperous so.'

'Thanks be to God, we are.'

He was a wandering beggar: they could not tell that what he wore had been a monk's habit once, or that a tonsure had further marked his calling. They would have considered him blasphemous if he had divulged that he was angry with

Our Lady, that he resented the mockery of this reward for his compliance in the past, that on his journey bitterness had spread in him. 'Am I your plaything?' he gruffly demanded as he trudged on and, hearing himself, was again ashamed.

He passed through a forest, so dark at its heart it might have been night. Hour upon hour it took before the trees began to dwindle and the faint light of another evening dappled the gloom. He passed that night on the forest's edge, covering himself again with undergrowth.

'I will go back,' he muttered in the morning, but knew immediately that this petulance was an empty threat: he would not find the way if he attempted to return; wild boars and wolves would come at night. Even though the gorse had drawn blood, he knew he was protected while he was obedient, for in the dark of the forest he had not once suffered from a broken branch spiking his head or face, had not once stumbled on a root.

So, testily, he went on. The hoar-frost that whitened grass and vegetation was lost within an hour each morning to the sun. St Sabas's day came, St Finnian's, St Lucy's, St Ammon's. In other years they had occurred in all weathers, but on Michael's journey it still did not rain. He cracked open nuts, searched where there was water for cresses and wild parsley. He remembered, on St Thomas's day, Luchan telling of Thomas's finger placed on the wound and of his cry of anguish as his doubt was exposed, and his Saviour's chiding. 'It is only that I cannot understand,' Michael pleaded, again begging for the solace of forgiveness.

Often he did not rest but walked on when darkness fell, and sometimes he did not eat. The strength to walk remained, but there was a lightness in his head and, going on, he wondered about his life, whether or not he had wasted the time given to him on earth. He begged at the door of a great house and was brought in, to warmth and food. The lady of the house came to the kitchen to pour wine for him and ask if he'd seen badgers and foxes the way he had come. He said he had. Her dark hair and the olive skin of her face put him in mind of Fódla once and that night, when he lay in a bed as comfortable as he had ever known, he thought about his childhood friend: her skin would be rough now, and lined, her hands ingrained from a lifetime's work. More anger was kindled in him; he was no longer penitent. Why should it have been that Fódla bore the children of another man, that she had come to belong to someone else, that he had been drawn away from her? His melancholy thoughts frightened him, seeming like a madness almost. Since first he had dreamed his holy dreams had there been some folly that controlled him, a silliness in his credulity? Had he been led into what Cathal called confusion's dance? Cathal would have spoken on that, Diarmaid too, and Ioin. There would have been their arguments and their concern, and the wisdom of Brother Beocca. But alone and lost in nowhere there was only a nagging that did not cease, a mystery that mocked and taunted, that made of him in his fifty-ninth year a bad-tempered child.

Mass was said in the house in the morning, and the lady of the house came to him when he was given breakfast.

'Do not hasten on,' she begged, 'if you do not have to. These days of the year, we would not wish to see you without a roof.'

Stay, she urged, until St Stephen's day, offering her hospitality with a smile touched by sorrow. She was a widow, he had heard in the kitchen.

They would clothe him, although it was not said. They would burn the old habit that was no longer recognizable as to its origin. He had told them nothing about himself; they had not asked.

'You are welcome in my house,' he heard the invitation repeated. 'And the weather may turn bitter.'

It would be pleasant to stay. There was the bed, the kitchen fireside. He had watched the spicing of beef the evening before; he had seen poultry hanging in the cold rooms, and fruits laid out in jars.

'I am not allowed to stay,' he said, and shook his head and was not pressed.

It was soon after he left the house, still in the same hour, that his cheerless mood slipped from him. As he walked away in the boots he had been given, he sensed with startling abruptness – not knowing why he did – that he had not failed himself, either as the young man he once had been or the old man he had become; and he knew that this journey was not the way to his death. Faithful to her prediction, the Virgin had not come to him again, but in a different way he saw her as she might have been before she was holy. He saw her taken aback by the angel's annunciation, and plunged into a confusion such as he had experienced himself. For her, there had been a journey too. For her, there had been tiredness and apprehension, and unkind mystery. And who could say there had not been crossness also?

Like blood flowing again, trust trickled back and Michael felt as he had when first he was aware he would survive among the rocks of his island. There was atonement in the urgency of his weary travail for three more days; and when the fourth day lightened he knew where he was.

The abbey was somewhere to the east, the pasture land ahead of him he had once walked. And closer, there was the hill on which so often he had watched over his father's sheep. There was the stream along which the alders grew, their branches empty of leaves now. No flock grazed the slopes of the hill, nor were there geese in the orchard, nor pigs rooting beneath the beech tree. But the small stone farmhouse was hardly changed.

There was no sound when he went nearer, and he stood for a moment in the yard, glancing about him at the closed doors of the outside houses, at the well and the empty byre. Grass grew among the roughly hewn stones that cobbled the surface beneath his feet. Ragwort and nettles withered in a corner. A roof had fallen in.

They answered his knock and did not know him. They gave him bread and water, two decrepit people he would not have recognized had he met them somewhere else. The windows of their kitchen were stuffed with straw to keep the warmth in. The smoke from the hearth made them cough. Their clothes were rags.

'It is Michael,' suddenly she said.

His father, blind, reached out his hand, feeling in the air. 'Michael,' he said also.

There was elation in their faces, joy such as Michael had never seen in faces anywhere before. The years fell back from them, their eyes were lit again with vigour in their happiness. A single candle burned in celebration of the day, its grease congealed, holding it to the shelf above the hearth.

Their land would not again be tilled; he was not here for that. Geese would not cry again in the orchard, nor pigs grub beneath the beech trees. For much less, and yet for more, he had been disturbed in the contentment of his solitude. So often he had considered the butterflies of his rocky fastness his summer angels, but if there were winter angels also they were here now, formless and unseen. No choirs sang, there was no sudden splendour, only limbs racked by toil in a smoky hovel, a hand that blindly searched the air. Yet angels surely held the cobweb of this mercy, the gift of a son given again.

Death of a Professor

The roomful of important men expectantly await the one whom another has already dubbed the party's ghost. In some, anticipation is disguised, in others it is a glint in an eye, a flushed cheek, the flicker of a smile that comes and goes. Within their disciplines it is their jealously possessed importance that keeps those gathered in the room going, but for once, this morning, their disciplines do not matter. Shafts of insult remain unlaunched, old scores can wait as the Master's Tio Pepe makes the rounds. Gossip is in command today.

'Oh, just a – a jape, they say?' little McMoran mutters, excusing cruelty with a word he has to search for. His sister's school stories of forty years ago were full of japes – *The Girls of the Chalet School, Jo Finds a Way, The Terrible Twins*. No point in carrying on about it, McMoran mutters also: they'll never find the instigator now. A bit of fun, still mischievously he adds.

Seeming almost twice McMoran's size, Linderfoot sniffs into his empty glass, his great pate shiny in bright winter light. Oh, meant as fun, he quite agrees. No joke, of course, if it comes your way. No joke to be called dead before your time.

'It hasn't come your way, though,' McMoran scratchily

155

points out, and wonders what the obituarists have composed already about this overweight, obtuse man, for he has always considered Linderfoot more than a little stupid even though he holds a Chair, which McMoran doesn't. Obedient, it would seem, to the devilment of some jesting or malicious student, four newspapers this morning have published their obituarists' tributes to the professor who has not yet arrived for the Master's midday drinks.

'Kind on the whole,' Quicke remarks to a colleague who does not respond, being one of several in the room who likes to keep a private counsel. 'Oh, kind, of course. No, I would not say less than kind.'

Grinning through bushy sideburns that spread on to his cheeks, Quicke offers variations of his thought, recalling an attack made on the historian Willet-Horsby after his death – disguised, of course, but none the less an attack. '1956. Unusual on an obituary page, but there you are.'

Quicke is the untidiest of the men in the room, his pink corduroy suit having gone without the attentions of an iron for many weeks, the jacket shabby, lapels touched here and there with High Table droppings. A virulent red tie – assertion of Quicke's political allegiance – does not quite hide the undone buttons of his checked lumberjack's shirt. He is a hairy, heavily made man, his facial features roughly textured, who in his sixties is still the *enfant terrible* of College junketings and gatherings such as this one.

'Ormston has taken it in his stride,' he finishes his observations now, guessing this to be far from so. 'He is a man of humour.'

'Ormston's nothing of the sort.' The tallest man in the room, skinny as a tadpole, Triller peers down at the Master's wife to contradict what both have overheard. Triller is courteous but given on occasion to sharpness, tweedily one of the old school, with a pipe that this midday remains unlit in the Master's drawing-room.

'It is a most appalling thing,' the Master's wife, the only woman in the room, asserts. 'I doubt that Professor Ormston will turn up.'

'You've had no word?'

'Not a thing.'

'Oh, then he'll come. Unlike him not to.'

'It's going too far, don't you think, this? Why is it that everything must go too far these days?'

'Your husband, I'm perfectly certain, intends to do what is necessary.'

The Master is lax, Triller's private view is. Tarred with the Sixties' brush, the Master long ago let the reins slip away. What better can be expected now? A show of strength is necessary, and Triller adds:

'Not for an instant do I doubt the Master's intention to supply it. How odd, though, that the victim should be Ormston.'

'I didn't myself realize Professor Ormston was unpopular. No, not at all.'

'He does not suck up.' Professor Triller glances briefly at Wirich's back and is pleased when the Master's wife acknowledges his allusion with one of her faint smiles. 'I don't suppose Ormston has ever worn leathers in his life.'

This elicits laughter, a tinkle in the noise of conversation. Though not attired so now, Wirich is given to leather – jackets and tight leather trousers, studded belts, occasionally a choker. He rides a motorcycle, a big Yamaha.

'Could this not simply be carelessness?' the Master's wife suggests. 'Newspapers have a way, these days, of being careless.'

'Not four different obituary departments, I'd have thought. I rather fear it was deliberate.'

Plump, with spectacles dangling, the Master's wife retorts that no matter how the unpleasantness has come about it is unacceptable in an older university. She's cross because what clearly excites her guests does not excite her, nor the Master himself. Something has been taken from them, she feels. Today should belong to them.

'I considered telephoning Ormston,' the Master reveals to the author of *Tribal Organization in the Karakoram Foothills* and to a classicist who considers the investigation of foothill tribes a waste of time. 'But then I rather thought that would simply highlight the thing, so I didn't.'

Nods greet this. They would have resisted telephoning too, a joint indication is, both men reflecting that the Master's role is not one they could ever take to, with irritating decisions endlessly to consider.

'I really am disturbed.' Given to booming, the Master lowers his voice to indicate the seriousness of his state. 'I truly am.'

Before his time, by as much as fifteen years, there was the business of Batchett's extra-mural lecture, and longer ago still the mocking of T. L. Hapgood, which now is in the annals, although no one in the Master's drawing-room this midday knew T. L. Hapgood in his lifetime or is aware of what he looked like. More recently, one morning, there was the delivery of a pig to Dr Kindly, and that same evening four dozen take-away pizzas. Batchett had presented himself at a famous public school to lecture to the Geographical Society on land lines, only to discover that not only had some sort of mid-term break emptied the school of his anticipated audience but that there was, in fact, no Geographical Society and never had been.

'The Hapgood riddle was never solved?' the Karakoram foothills man hazards. 'I've never known.'

'No, they didn't get to the bottom of it. Years later, identities often surface after such nuisances, but none did then. Some disaffected bunch.'

The bunch who took against T. L. Hapgood – by general consent because his sarcasm hurt – based their jape on the professor's disdain for the stream of consciousness in the literature of his time. Other academics were written to in Professor Hapgood's name, announcing his authorship of a forthcoming study of James Joyce's life and works. *I feel my task will be incomplete and greatly lacking without the inclusion of your views on the great Irishman, and in particular, perhaps, on his subtle and enlightening use of what we have come to call the 'stream of consciousness'. Anything from a paragraph to thirty or so pages would be welcome from your pen, with prompt reward either in cheque form or our own good claret, whichever is desired. I am most reluctant to go to press without your voice, inimitable in its perception and its sagacity.* For eighteen months Professor Hapgood received contributions from Europe, America, Japan and the antipodes. Later, demands for reimbursement became abusive.

'I didn't know Ormston in his youth wanted to be a cabinet-maker,' the classicist remarks. 'It said that in one of them this morning.'

'Affectionately, though,' the Master hurriedly interjects. 'The point was affectionately made.'

'Oh yes, affectionately.'

Historians and philosophers and breezy sociologists, promoters of literature and language, of medieval lore and the Internet, they stand about and talk or do not talk. In different ways the diversion draws them from their shells, even those who have decided that comment on any matter can be a giveaway. Some wonder about the absent victim, others about his younger wife – a flibbertigibbet in Triller's view, the price you pay for beauty. To McMoran it seems like fate's small revenge that Ormston should be struck down before his time: his own wife has long ago given in to dowdiness and fat.

At twenty-five past twelve there is a lull in the drawing-room conversations, occurring as if for a reason, although there isn't one. For a moment only Quicke's rather high voice can be heard, repeating to someone else that Ormston is a man of humour. A snigger is inadequately suppressed.

'My dear, there are empty glasses,' the Master's wife murmurs in her husband's ear.

As he looks about him, wondering where he left the decanter, the conversational lull seems not to have been adventitious after all, but a portent. The doorbell sounds. Professor Ormston has come at last.

*

Someone once said – the precise source of a much-repeated observation long ago lost – that in her heyday Vanessa Ormston's beauty recalled Marilyn Monroe's. Over the years, inevitably has come the riposte that she still possesses the film star's brain. Photographs show a smiling girl with bright fair hair, slender to the point of slightness, her features lit with the delicate beauty of a child. At forty-eight – younger by sixteen years than her husband – she seems thin rather than slender and has retained her beauty to the same degree that the flowers she presses between the leaves of books have. Ormston's wife – as she is often designated among her husband's colleagues – has a passion for flowers. Significance has been found in her preservation of blooms beyond their prime, the venom of envy spilt a little in college cloisters or at High Table.

Very early on the morning of the Master's sherry do – that racy term racily approved in academe – Vanessa read the obituary of her husband, whom ten minutes ago she had left alive in the twin bed next to hers. Arrested by the grainy photograph – head and shoulders, caught at Commencements five years ago – her instinct was to hurry upstairs to make sure everything was all right, that time had not played tricks on her. Was it somehow another day? Had amnesia kindly erased the facts of tragedy? But then she heard her husband's footfall and his early-morning cough. Mistily, she read – a revelation – that he was well loved by his students.

She read that he was 'distinguished in his small world' and knew he would not care for that. None of them recognized that his world was small.

The electric kettle came to the boil while Vanessa read on; and then, alarmed anew, she hurried upstairs. He was propped up on his pillows after his brief absence from the bed, what showed of him almost a replica of the photographed head and shoulders on the fawn Formica surface of the kitchen table. 'Won't be a tick,' she managed to get out and hurried off again to make their seven o'clock tea, the tray prepared the night before, gingersnap biscuits in the round tin with 'The Hay Wain' on it. The newspaper should accompany all this, his turn to scan it then.

Vanessa lost her head, as in difficult moments she tended to. She could not possibly hand the paper to him and wait for him to arrive at his recorded death. His companions on the page – no doubt correctly there – were a backing singer of a pop group, a bishop, born in Stockport, and a lieutenant colonel. *Professor A. R. Ormston*, it said, the space allocated to him less than that of the others, less particularly than the backing singer's. The bishop's photograph was small, but generous text made up for that; the lieutenant colonel married Anne Nancy Truster-Ede in 1931 and lost an arm in Cyprus. Gazing at his soldier's brave old eyes and the bishop's murky likeness, the raddled babyface of the singer, metal suspended from lobe and nostril, Vanessa again said to herself that she could not possibly commit this cruelty. Being crammed into what space remained was horrible.

The obituaries were on the inside of the last page. There

had been a time when the paperboy jammed the paper into the letter-box, tearing that page quite badly. *Please leave the newspapers on the window-sill,* her husband had instructed on a square of cardboard which he suspended from the brass hall-door handle. He kept the square of cardboard by him, displaying it each time the paperboy changed.

Vanessa tore the bottom of the page and bundled away what she could not bring herself to reveal. She dropped the ball of paper into the waste-bucket beneath the sink, pushing it well down, under potato peelings and a soup tin. Then she carried the tray upstairs.

'We need to hang out your notice again,' she said, pouring tea and adding milk. 'It's a different boy.'

'What boy's that, dear?'

'The one with the papers.'

What on earth else could I do? she wildly asked herself, dipping a gingersnap into her tea. She had needed time to think, but now that she had it could think of nothing. Her worried features, private behind the cover of the magazine that had been delivered also, were a blankness that filled eventually with a consideration of the consequences of her subterfuge. It did not occur to her that this was anything but an error in a single newspaper. More on her mind was that her protection could not possibly last, that when the moment of truth arrived no explanation could soften the harshness of an obituarist's mistake. She might have tried to speak, to lead on gently to a confession, but still she could not.

'Whatever's a stealth fighter?' came an enquiry from the other bed, the question answered almost as soon as it was asked. An F117 Stealth Fighter was an aeroplane, she was told, and also told that there was going to be trouble with the postal unions, and then that there was not much news today. 'Oh, little do you know!' her own voice cried, though only to herself. She turned the pages of her magazine, seeing nothing of them. Her desperation misled her: friends and colleagues would rally round in humane conspiracy, their instinct to protect, as hers had been. When letters arrived from those who could not know the truth she would reply, explaining. They would, in the nature of things, be addressed to her. That some undergraduate, when the new term began, might say, 'Sir, surely you are dead?' did not enter Vanessa's bewildered thoughts. He was well loved by his students, after all. They, too, would surely respect his dignity.

But minutes later, when Professor Ormston's wife stood in the bedroom with her dressing-gown and nightdress slipped off, the moment before her underclothes every morning felt cold on her skin, she knew she had again done the wrong thing, as so often she had in her marriage and in her life. And as so often also, she had compounded it by creating an unreal wonderland: they would take pleasure, all of them, in this amusement.

'What shall today bring?' the Professor wondered from his bed, words familiar in the bedroom at this time.

She thought to tell him then. She could have gone to him half dressed, and offered consolation with her young wife's body. 'I am ridiculous,' instead her own voice echoed, soundless in the room, ridiculous because she did not have the courage to cause pain.

She boiled his egg and made his toast. She heated milk for their coffee. To come were the leisurely hours of this Saturday morning, while still he would not know. And hopelessly again she wondered why, for once, it should not be different, why at the Master's sherry do they should not be merciful.

*

'This matter shall be dealt with,' is the Master's greeting. 'Have no doubt on that score.'

He says no more, only nods through what he takes to be Ormston's embarrassment but is, in fact, bewilderment. It seems to the Master that Ormston intends to ride the storm, disdaining comment. And in that, of course, he must be honoured. 'Is this what's called insouciance?' McMoran mutters, struck also by Ormston's calm.

Alone in a corner a medievalist, Kellfittard, regards Ormston with a distaste that reaches into hatred. 'The Quicke and the dead,' Kellfittard hears coming from his left when for a moment the man declared to be no longer alive is in the company of the pinkly corduroyed professor. Kellfittard cares for neither of them, but has more reason to dislike the one he imagined until an hour ago had left his wife a widow. Kellfittard's bachelor status has everything to do with Vanessa Ormston, who is of an age with him and wasted, so he believes, on a dry old man. Dry himself, he is one of the professors who are economical with their utterances, an inclination in him that played against his chances where Vanessa was concerned, allowing his rival to get in first. Hours ago in his cheerless college rooms he gazed in disbelief and wonder, and then in pure delight, at the likeness on the obituary page, went out to buy the three other newspapers he guessed might carry the same happy tidings, and there they were. Fantasies began at once: theatre visits with Vanessa Ormston, quiet dinners at The Osteria, a discreet weekend, and in Salzburg before the autumn term began the honeymoon that should have taken place years ago. It wasn't until he arrived at the Master's house that Kellfittard realized some prankster had been at work.

Quicke's donkey roar reaches him in his corner. It mocks him, as the faces all around him do – McMoran's wizened, Linderfoot's a blob of fat, the one that has been to the Karakoram foothills sunburnt, Wirich's beaky, the Master's square and heavy, Triller's long and tidy. Kellfittard himself shares with the man who nineteen years ago snatched beauty from him a pallor without a trace of pink, and rimless spectacles. Both men are grey-haired; both are sparely made. In the course of his morning's thoughts it seemed rational to Kellfittard that, in marrying again, a wife would choose, the second time, a physical repetition. Though in no other way, those same thoughts adamantly insisted, was there a similarity.

'Impossible to know how it was done. One of our names taken in vain, I have no doubt.'

It is Linderfoot who makes that pronouncement, approaching Kellfittard in his chummy way. What Linderfoot maintains – idiotically, it seems to Kellfittard – is that some undergraduate has simply acted a part on the telephone, proffering the news of a professor's death.

'Your name or mine,' Linderfoot presses, 'would seem to have been enough.'

'No,' another man joins in to say. 'That would not have been enough.'

'Then what?' Linderfoot purses his big lips as if to whistle, his habit when a conversation palls. The man who has butted in says:

'This was done from within a news agency. It must have been.'

'A *news* agency?'

'One of Ormston's old students. Forgiveness does not come cheaply always.'

'But Ormston –'

'We all offend.'

'Ormston appears to be pretending it hasn't happened.' Kellfittard breaks his silence with that. He does not say he rejoiced to know the man was dead. He does not believe that he himself in any way offends his students, but he keeps that back also.

'Extraordinary,' Linderfoot interjects, pursing his lips again. 'Extraordinary.'

It is known to the others, but not to Linderfoot – who takes no interest in such matters – that Kellfittard feels he should have married Vanessa Ormston, that he has married no one else because a passion has lingered. It's understandable, in Linderfoot's opinion, that Ormston should choose to ignore the embarrassment of what has happened to him. He blunders about the room, seeking other conversations, unaware of the prevailing disappointment that Ormston has not appeared among them a broken man, that there has been this anticlimax.

'An inside job,' Quicke remarks eventually, determined to exact something from the let-down. Leaving the house with Ormston, he offers his opinion as they make their way on the Master's wide garden path. 'On the media front, an inside job, so they are saying now.'

He touches one nostril and then the other with a red spotted handkerchief, causing Ormston to look away. Quicke's manner implies particular comradeship between the two, a lowered tone suggests concern. The comradeship does not exist, the concern's unreal.

'What are you talking about?' Ormston asks and in a roundabout way, the information larded with commiseration, he learns of what has occurred.

*

Passing on his left the grey-brown stone of porters' lodge and deeply recessed library windows, Ormston remembers the torn back page of his morning paper. The face of the pop-group singer, which briefly he glanced at, is as briefly repeated in his recall. What was missing from that page was what was left hanging when the Master said the matter would be dealt with. The Master's wife was awkward in her greeting, McMoran smug. Triller's vague air disguised something else; Wirich stared; Linderfoot was excited; Kellfittard looked the other way. Every one of them knows.

As others already have, Ormston knits together an explanation that is similar to theirs except in detail. When he was young himself an unpopular Senior Dean suffered the indignity of being approached by a police constable, following information that confused his identity with a draper's elderly assistant who hung around public lavatories. A youth called Tottle was sent down for that; and Ibbs and Churchman suffered the same fate less than a term later for stealing the Master's clothing, confining him miserably when he should have been delivering the Hardiman lecture in the presence of a member of the Royal Family. All one year there'd been a spate of that kind of thing, chamber pots on spires, false charges laid, old Purser's bicycle dismantled more than a dozen times.

Why should he be a victim now? He is not arrogant that he's aware of, or aloof among his students; he does not seek to put them in their place. Lacking the ambition of his colleagues, he is a scholar as scholars used to be, learned in an old-fashioned sense. Has all this jarred and irritated without his knowing? Still walking slowly, Professor Ormston shakes his head. He is not a fool, of course he would have sensed unpopularity.

Noticing the green and black hanging sign of the St Boniface public house, he considers entering it and a moment later does so instead of passing by. He has rarely in his life been in a public house, maybe a dozen times in all, he estimates as the swing doors close behind him. Blue plush banquettes along the walls are marked with cigarette burns, as are the low tables arranged in front of them, each with a glass ashtray advertising a brand of beer and small round mats bearing similar insignia. Unwashed glasses have been collected and are still on trays; busy ten minutes ago with Saturday-morning trade, the place is empty now.

'Sir?' a man behind the bar greets Professor Ormston, looking up from a plate of minced meat with a topping of potato.

'Might I have a glass of whisky?'

'You could of course, sir.'

Warmly steaming, smeared with tomato sauce, the food smells of the grease it has been cooked in. On a radio somewhere a disc jockey is gabbling incomprehensibly.

'Would I make that a double, sir?'

As if aware that his customer is unused to public-house measures, the barman holds the glass up to display how little whisky there is in it.

'Yes, please do.'

'Decent enough bit of weather.'

'Yes, it is.'

'There you go, sir.'

'Thanks.'

He pays and takes the drink to one of the tables by the windows. 'Kind,' was how Quicke put it; all four obituarists were kind in Quicke's opinion. 'Quite right, of course.' And he was able to nod, not up to pretending aloud that yes, the notices were kind enough. A dare, Quicke said, young men have dares. They think up these things and the one who is eventually in a position to do so sees something through. A bet it might have been, and probably was. There'd be apologies from all four editors, Quicke was certain about that.

A child appears behind the bar, only the top of her head

visible. The man tells her to go away, but then he reaches for a glass and pours a Pepsi Cola into it while continuing to eat. He tells the girl she'll be the ruin of him.

'This'll make me drunk,' Professor Ormston tells himself, whisky on top of Tio Pepe before lunch. And yet he wants to stay here. The newspaper beside the trays of unwashed glasses on the bar is not the kind that has obituaries. Again the torn page stirs in his recall, only half of the backing singer there, the name of the army colonel not known to him, as the bishop's wasn't either. Of course a popular entertainer took precedence. The way things are these days, that stands to reason.

'I'm sorry,' he says at the bar after he has sat for a while longer, apologizing because the man hasn't finished his food. But the man is cheerful, Irish by the sound of him. Professor Ormston has read somewhere that the Irish make good publicans, a touch of the blarney not out of place.

'Sure, and what am I here for, sir? Wouldn't I be negligent to eat me dinner with a man going thirsty?'

'Thank you so much.'

He carries the replenished glass back to where he has been sitting. *Survived by his wife, Vanessa.* It would have said that, Vanessa mentioned once. No children, acquaintances of long ago would notice. And students who did not know he'd ever married would be surprised, he not being the sort, they might in their day have assumed. When they took her on as secretary in the department there had hardly been enough work to justify it and she was bored at first, until it was suggested she should be shared with McMoran. When she left, three years ago, it was because she didn't like McMoran.

She has done what she thought best. He knows that in her; and sipping more whisky, he tries to understand. Apart altogether from McMoran's spikiness, she had never been happy in the department, as later she confessed. 'You think this girl's up to it?' he asked when they first considered her, not even noticing her beauty then. This city, not a human attribute, was what he'd thought of when he thought of beauty, the grey-brown columns and façades, carved figures in their niches, the lamplight coming on in winter. Seven hours have passed, he calculates: she came up with the tea and gingersnaps, prevaricating although prevarication does not come naturally to her.

Another man comes in, who doesn't have to order what he wants. The barman knows and pours a bottle of Adnams' beer. 'Floating Voter,' the barman says. 'You'll get him at nines.'

The others kept it to themselves when she left the department, unable to criticize her because she was his wife. Mc-Moran muttered something, feeling more let down because he had relied on her more, but what he said wasn't audible. It doesn't interest any of them that she is happier now, that she has given her life up to her flowers and to her hospital charity work, amusing children while they wait on cystic-fibrosis days, or children undergoing leukaemia treatment, or hole-in-the heart children. 'I don't know how she does it,' he might have said, but never has because they wouldn't be interested in the charity work of someone's wife. She wanted children; he could not give her them.

The trawl through his life that she has withheld from him would not, of course, record that. Nor would it touch upon his occasional testiness, his cold appraisal of examination answers, the orderly precision that enhances his work and affects him as a husband, the melancholy that comes from nowhere. Other human-interest decoration might enliven a drab account, with liberties taken for the casual reader. *His wife was younger by sixteen years* most certainly would not be written. Nor *as lovely in her day as Marilyn Monroe.*

The whisky has dried his mouth. In the Master's drawing-room he would have seemed a figure of silliness, not saying anything: those of them who have wives would now be passing that across their lunch tables. They'd be amused to know that he is surreptitiously drinking in a public house.

*

The house is silent. Wintry sunshine dwindles in the kitchen, on the places laid at the oval table, each of the two plates of tongue covered with another plate, for the sun has made the window a haven for the last of autumn's flies. A salad, the oil and vinegar dressing not yet added, is covered also.

Whoever the perpetrators are, Vanessa feels she belongs with them, that she has added something to their cruelty. 'I couldn't think, I didn't know what I was doing': all that is ready, and has been for longer than the food she has prepared. 'Panic,' she must also say, for that word belongs. 'I went all blank.' No need to say a wife should have the courage to bear bad news.

He'll know because it will, of course, have all come out; and then he'll see her reddened eyes and know the rest as well. A nest of vipers the Master and his simpering wife gather round them on these occasions. Who has a chance in a nest of vipers?

'My God!' Vanessa's mother exclaimed in open horror when, nineteen years ago almost to the month, she learned of her daughter's engagement to a fusty academic who was just old enough to be her father. 'My God!' she said again after their first encounter, when Vanessa brought him for the weekend to her mother's flat. 'Has he money?' she asked, unable to find some other reason for what she termed an unattractive marriage. 'Just what he earns,' Vanessa replied, and two months later married him.

His key turns in the hall-door Yale. While waiting for him, it has occurred to Vanessa that there would be the other newspapers. She has imagined him in a newsagent's, giving the right money because he likes to if he can, taking the papers to where he can peruse them undisturbed.

The hall door bangs softly; he does not call her name. There's the pause that means he's hanging up his overcoat and scarf, the papers placed on the table beneath the picture of a café scene. There are his footsteps then.

'I have to tell you,' her husband says, 'that I believe I'm drunk.'

His voice is quiet, the words not slurred. He does not look drunk; he is the same. He doesn't smile, but then he often doesn't when he comes in. 'A sobersides,' her mother said. 'Wizened,' she added, although that wasn't true.

'I looked in at the St Boniface,' he says. 'Understandably, I believe.'

'I'm awfully sorry.'

'Oh Lord, it's not your fault.'

'I –'

'I know, I know.'

'I couldn't think.'

'I couldn't when I heard, myself.'

'They mentioned it?'

'Quicke couldn't resist a little mention. It didn't matter. Sooner or later someone would.'

'Yes.'

'The culprits will be exposed, the Master's view is. Of course he's wrong.'

'You don't seem drunk in the least.' Relief has slipped through Vanessa during these exchanges. For a reason that is obscure to her, and for the first time since she turned the pages of the newspaper while waiting for the early-morning kettle to boil, she feels that nothing is as terrible as it seemed in those awful moments.

'To the best of my knowledge I have never in my life been drunk before. The man poured three double whiskies, and that on top of sherry.'

She lifts the plates that cover their cold meat. She stirs the oil and vinegar, shakes the salad about when she has added a few spoonfuls, then pours on the rest. Perhaps they'll go away, Vanessa's thought is, perhaps he'll take an early retirement, as one of them so unexpectedly did last year. She'd pack up at once, she wouldn't hesitate. Liguria, or Sansepolcro, where his favourite paintings are. Hers, too, they have become. 'I could live here happily,' he has said, over coffee in Sansepolcro.

'I can tell you how this has happened,' he says. 'If you would care to know.'

'Panic,' she begins to say, and ceases when he shakes his head, grey hair as smooth as a helmet.

'An act of compassion,' he corrects.

'But it was stupid. To try to suppress what cannot be suppressed –'

'Why cannot an act of compassion be a stupid one? I can tell you,' he repeats exactly, 'how this has happened. If you would care to know.'

'Some horrid, wretched student.'

'I am not the sort to inspire a grudge. I am too shadowy and grey, too undramatic. I annoy too little, I do not attack.'

She watches the buttering of a piece of baguette, the knife laid down, the meticulous loading of tongue and salad on to a fork, the smear of mustard. She pours his coffee; he likes it with his food at this time of day, with French bread in particular, he has often said. My God, Vanessa thinks, it might be true. He might not be here now.

'Imagine Kellfittard opening his paper this morning. Imagine his happy hour or two.'

For a moment she is confused, thinking he means Kellfittard is responsible for this. He says, 'And then the rug pulled out from under him. Generations have suffered from Kellfittard's wit. It passes for that, you know. So much we fusties say passes for wit.'

'But you –'

'They would not mind about me. Whoever they are who

got this going would not think twice about reaping me in before I'm due. What's famous here is Kellfittard's abiding passion for someone else's wife.'

The last time Kellfittard stopped to talk to her yesterday's garlic was on his breath. Stopping to talk to her has always been his ploy, and smiling in a secretive way – as if, by doing so, secrets are created.

'Fall-guy, do they call it?' she hears her husband say. 'I am the fall-guy.'

He has winkled out the truth, sitting in the public house he gave the name of, which she has often passed. The truth doesn't make much difference, and certainly is no consolation. Yet for her older husband it had to be established, if only because it's there somewhere. Students who are no longer students have got their own back. He is an incidental figure, and so is she.

'Well, that is that,' he says. 'Four notices in all, Quicke said. Space to spare on a Saturday.'

'There will be letters.'

'Oh, and apologies will be printed. So Quicke says too.'

Something in his tone, or in what he has said, causes her to realize that she was wrong when she imagined him buying the newspapers. He has not done so. He asks about the coffee and she says Kenya.

He nods. The coffee's good, he says. The other matter's over, he does not add, but Vanessa knows it is. Once Kellfittard gave her a box of chocolates, Bendicks' Peppermints because he knew she liked them. 'I bought these by mistake,' he said, the lie so damaging the gesture that the gesture lost its point. It would have been silly not to accept them.

'Linderfoot's put on another stone, I'd say. How fortunate the wives are to be left at home!'

His wisdom was what she loved when first she loved him, when she was still a girl. She called it that, though only to herself. Not brains, they all had brains. Not skill. Not knowing everything, for they knew less than they imagined. His wisdom is almost indefinable, what a roadworker might have, a cinema usher or a clergyman, or a child. Her mother would not understand, and he himself would deny that he is wise. Of course the papers are not on the hall table; of course he hasn't read a word – the subtle slights wrapped up as worthiness, and qualities he did not possess made his because it is the thing to do, all of valediction's clichés.

'No, no, a blunder,' she hears him say when the telephone rings, the first time it has today, the house of mourning left to itself until this moment. 'No, most ridiculous,' he says. 'I'm sorry if I startled you.'

He laughs, replacing the receiver, and Vanessa does not say she loves him, although she wants to. Absurd, to have thought of hiding away in Italy, packing everything up, leaving for ever his beautiful city just because they have been involved in someone else's hoax.

He has worn the better of the two, Vanessa reflects. Age in his features was always there; her beauty loses a little every day. 'I love your wisdom,' she wants to say, but still is shy to use that word, fearing a display of her naïvety would make her foolish.

'My dear,' he murmurs in the calmness they have reached, and holds her as he did the day he first confessed his adoration. It is the wedding of their differences that protects them, steadfast in the debris of the storm.

Against the Odds

Mrs Kincaid decided to lie low. There had been a bit of bother, nothing much but enough to cause her to change her address. From time to time she was obliged to do so.

She wondered about Portrush. It was May, which meant that the holiday accommodation would still be available at low-season terms. She wondered about Cushendall, which she would have preferred because she liked the air there, but only three years had passed since her last visit and somehow three years didn't feel quite long enough. Cushendun, Ballygalley, Portstewart, Ardglass, Bangor, Kilkeel: Mrs Kincaid had breathed the air in all of them.

This time, though, she decided on an inland town. She knew many of these also, Armagh and Lisburn in particular, but Ballymena, Magherafelt, Lurgan and Portadown almost as well. She was a Belfast woman herself, but long ago had made all the territory of the Six Counties her business ground. Only once, in 1987, had she strayed outside the North of Ireland, taking the Larne crossing to Stranraer, then travelling on to Glasgow, an episode in her life she regretted and preferred not to dwell upon. Equally regretted was a suspended sentence in the Derry courts in 1981, since it had ruled out as a place to do business in a city she was particularly fond of.

Mrs Kincaid – with no claim to that name other than her occasional use of it – was just over eleven stone, and tall. Although well covered, she gave no impression of plumpness; no bloated or sagging flesh seemed superfluous beneath her clothes. Her arms were sturdy, her legs looked strong. In her own opinion her biggish face was something she got away with, no feature in it particularly objectionable, neither a fallen-away chin nor protruding teeth. Modest in her dress, careful not to overdo her use of perfume and make-up, she was sixty years old, admitting to fifty-one. Her easy smile worked wonders.

'Well, isn't that great?' she remarked to the driver of the Ulsterbus that was taking her to the inland town she had finally chosen, one she neither knew nor was known in. Her display of elation as she entered the bus had to do with the declaration of peace in the Six Counties. A double cease-fire had been announced in the thirty years' war that was not called a war; politicians from within the North of Ireland and from London and Dublin, advisers from America, had drawn up a long agenda that had since been agreed to by referendum on both sides of the Border. Mrs Kincaid had not herself suffered more than inconvenience during the years of conflict; the trouble in her life had been a personal one. Yet the havoc that occurred with such weary repetition and for so long had naturally impinged; she would be glad to see its end.

'Great?' the bus driver responded to her optimism.

'The peace.'

'There's maybe something in their bits of paper.' Nonchalantly, the driver turned on the ignition. Windscreen wipers lumbered across the curved glass in front of him, clearing away a few drops of rain. 'We'll see,' he said, a reminder in his tone that whatever agreements had been reached, whatever pledges given, there were gunmen who had not gone away, who still possessed their armoury and were used to calling the tune. 'We'll see,' he said again.

'Hope for the best.'

'Aye.'

'Isn't it cold, though, for May? Whenever I looked out first thing I said you'll be needing your wool, Mabel.'

The bus driver agreed that the weather was unseasonable before starting his engine. Mrs Kincaid passed on to a seat. She never liked leaving Belfast. Its streets were hers, its intonations always a pleasure to hear again when she returned from an exile never made through choice. The bombs that had battered its buildings, blown its motor-cars to pieces, maimed and killed its citizens, had never, in thirty years, caused her to wish to live elsewhere. Child of a Belfast boarding-house, she had salted away the wealth that property had fetched when she inherited it, only later to be parted from her gains, which was the personal circumstance that had coloured her life since.

She sat alone on the bus, her two brown suitcases on the rack above her. As always, she travelled light. Rented rooms with furniture supplied were what she liked, someone else's taste. She lived in that way, and although she guessed that in the town she was going to there wouldn't be a soul who did so too, she would manage not to stand out. Not yet composed,

whatever story came to her on her journey would see to that
for her.

*

Blakely crushed the peas beneath his fork, then mixed them
into a mush of potato and gravy. There was one piece of
meat left, its size calculated to match what was left of the
potatoes and peas. Since first being on his own he had got
into this way of eating, of gauging forkfuls in advance, of
precisely combining the various items on his plate. It was a
substitute for conversation, for invariably, these days, Blakely
ate alone.

Six days a week he drove in from the farm and sat down
at the same table in Hirrel's Café, never looking at a menu but
taking whatever was on specially for that day. On Sundays he
sat down with the Reverend Johnston in the manse, having
brought with him whatever eggs he could spare, or butter-
milk, which the Reverend Johnston was partial to, once a
month a turkey. In December he supplied Hirrel's with
turkeys also.

The *Belfast Telegraph*, folded and propped up against two
Yorkshire Relish bottles, was full of the recent political devel-
opments and the prospect for the future. Fourteen years ago
Blakely's wife and daughter had been killed in error, a bomb
attached to a car similar in make and colour to the would-be
victim's, the registration number varying by only a single
digit. Promptly, he had received an apology, a telephone call
of commiserations that sounded genuine. Two wreaths were
sent.

He pushed his knife and fork to the side of the plate, and a few minutes later Mrs Hirrel brought him a plate of rhubarb and custard and a pot of tea. He thanked her, folding the newspaper away. The men of violence were still in charge, no doubt about it. He'd said that to Mrs Hirrel the time the cease-fires were predicted, and she'd agreed with him. They'd talked about it for a long while; today, as yesterday and the day before, there was nothing left to say on the subject. Mrs Hirrel remarked instead that the rhubarb was all young shoots, grown under plastic, the first that had come up out the back. 'See to that woman, Nellie,' she called out to her waitress, for a woman had entered the café, bringing with her a stream of bitterly cold air.

All the tables were taken, as they always were at this time. Shop people came to Hirrel's at lunchtime, commercial travellers took advantage of being in the town in the middle of the day. Toomey from the Northern Bank was always there, with the lady clerk he was doing a line with. Van drivers, occasionally a lorry driver, looked in.

'Can you wait a wee minute?' Nellie enquired of the newcomer. 'There's several finishing up.'

'D'you know who that is, Mr Blakely?' Mrs Hirrel asked him, and he said he didn't, and Mrs Hirrel said nor did she. 'Would she sit there a minute with you while you drink your tea?'

Sometimes this happened because of the empty chair opposite him. He never minded. Travellers in drapery or hardware items would fall into conversation with him, giving him some idea of the current ups and downs of the commercial world, usually asking him what line he was in himself.

'Are you sure?' Led to the table, Mrs Kincaid was hesitant before she sat down. 'I wouldn't want to butt in on you.'

'You're doing rightly,' Blakely reassured her. He was a nervous man with strangers and often expressed himself not quite as he meant to in order to get out any words at all. His tea was hot and he would have liked to pour it on to the saucer. But that wouldn't do in Hirrel's.

'Homey,' Mrs Kincaid remarked, looking around her at a familiar aspect – the laminate tabletops, cheap knives and forks, plates of bread and butter, faces intent on mastication, a toothpick occasionally spearing trapped shreds: many times she had frequented cafés like this. The man opposite her at least had taken off his cap, which often men didn't when they ate in such places. He had tufty grey hair cut short and a lean, narrow face with a deep flush in both cheeks. A healthy-looking, outside man, well enough dressed, with a collar and tie. In Mrs Kincaid's childhood if a man not wearing a collar and tie came to the boarding-house after a room he was turned away at once.

'Isn't it chilly today, though?' she remarked, noticing that a plate of rhubarb and custard had been finished quite tidily, a little left behind, spoon and fork kept together. Late fifties, she put him down as; fingernails a little grimed but nothing to write home about.

'There's a few more days of it,' he said, and then the waitress was there, asking her what she'd like, saying the mutton was finished. Mrs Kincaid ordered a plate of bread and butter, and tea.

'Have we peace at last?' she asked and the man replied civilly enough that you wouldn't know. His own opinion was that there was a long way to go, and she could feel him being careful about how he put it, in how he chose his words. Not knowing about her, not knowing which foot she dug with, as her father used to say, he held back. He poured himself another cup of tea, added milk and stirred in sugar, two spoonfuls of granulated.

'Ach, it's been going on too long,' she said.

'Maybe it's the end so.'

He folded his newspaper into a side pocket of his jacket. The jacket was of dark tweed and needed a press, a thread hanging down where a button had come off. You could tell from his way with the waitress that he was a regular. He counted out the money for his bill and left a 5p piece and some coppers as a tip. 'Good day,' he said before he went to pay at the counter.

From force of habit rather than anything else, Mrs Kincaid continued to wonder about Blakely after he'd gone. She wondered if he could be a road surveyor, since something about him reminded her of a road surveyor she'd once briefly known. She imagined him with a road gang, a smell of tar in the air, fresh chippings still pale on the renovated surface. Then Mrs Kincaid reminded herself that she wasn't here to interest herself in a man she didn't know, far from it. She had left her two suitcases in the newsagent's shop where the bus had put her down. When she'd had something to eat and had made enquiries she'd go back and collect them.

'Try Bann Street,' the waitress said. 'There's a few that lets rooms there.'

*

Leave it, Mrs Kincaid warned herself again when she noticed Blakely coming out of Hirrel's Café four days later, repeating her reminder to herself that she was not here for anything like that. She'd stay a month, she had decided; from experience a month was long enough for any bit of trouble to quieten. Talk of solicitors' letters, of walking straight round to a police station, threats of this and that, all simmered away to nothing when a little time went by. Frayed tempers mended, pride came to terms with whatever foolishness she'd taken advantage of in the way of business. Not that much had mended in her own case, not that pride had ever recovered from the dent it had received, but her own case was different and always had been. Eighty-four thousand pounds the boarding-house had realized in 1960, more like ten times that it would be now. 'We'd put the little enterprise in your name,' the man she'd thought of as her fiancé had said. 'No hanky-panky.' But somehow in the process of buying what he always called the little enterprise the eighty-four thousand had slipped out of her name. Soon after that it disappeared and he with it. The little enterprise it was to purchase was a bookmaker's in Argyle Street, an old bookie retiring, two generations of goodwill. A chain took it over a couple of months later.

These days Mrs Kincaid did her best to take the long view, telling herself that what had happened was like a death and that you couldn't moan about a death for ever, not even to yourself. In her business activities she did not seek vengeance but instead sought to accumulate what was rightfully hers, keeping her accounts in a small red notebook, always with the hope that one day she would not have to do so, that her misfortune in the past would at last free her from its thrall.

Walking against a steady east wind on the day she saw Blakely for the second time, she recalled his lean face very clearly, his tufty hair, the hanging thread on his jacket where a button had come off. He'd be a bachelor or a widower, else he wouldn't be taking his dinner in a café every day. You could tell at once the foot he dug with, as decent a Protestant foot as her own, never a doubt about that.

The room she had taken – not in Bann Street but above a butcher's shop in Knipe Street – smelt of meat and suet. She had an electric ring to cook on, a sink for the washing of clothes and dishes, lavatory and bathroom a flight up. There was a television, a gas fire, a single bed under the window, and when she fried something on the electric ring the butchery smell disappeared for a while. Mrs Kincaid had been in worse places.

She brought back from the shops a bar of Kit-Kat, *Woman's Own*, *Hello!*, *The Lady*, and a film magazine. She ate the chocolate bar, read a story about a late flowering of romance, made tea, slipped out of her skirt and blouse, slept, and dreamed she had married a clergyman to whom she'd once sold back the letters he'd written her. When she woke she washed herself, fried rashers and an egg, and went out again.

She sat alone at a table in the bar of Digby's Hotel, listening to tunes of the fifties, all of which she was familiar with.

Occasionally someone smiled at her, a man or a woman, the girl behind the bar, but generally they just went by. She heard talk about a dance. She would have gone on her own when she was younger, but those days were over now. She drank vodka with no more than a colouring of port in it, which was her tipple. She bought a packet of cigarettes, although as a general rule she didn't smoke any more. She wasn't going to be able to resist what had been put in her path: she knew that perfectly.

She knew it again when she woke up in the middle of the night and lay for a while awake in the darkness. The smell from the shop below had come back, and when she dropped back into sleep she dreamed that the man she had met in the café was in butcher's clothes, separating lamb chops with a cleaver.

*

There was a traveller on his own by the table at the window, but that was the smallest table in the café and he had his samples' case on the other chair, out of the way of people passing. Otherwise, Blakely's was the only table that wasn't shared.

'Only she said go on over,' the same woman who'd shared it with him before said.

'You're welcome. Sure, there's nowhere else.'

'Isn't that the bad news?' She nodded at the headline in his paper. A taxi-driver had been shot dead the evening before, the first murder since the cease-fires.

'Aye,' Blakely said. 'It is that.'

She was dressed as she'd been before, in shades of fawn and brown – a skirt and cardigan, cream blouse, under the coat she'd taken off. There was a brooch, made to look like a flower, in her blouse.

'The plate's hot, Mr Blakely,' Nellie warned, placing roast beef and potatoes and cabbage in front of him. She wiped the edge of the plate where gravy had left a residue.

'Bread and butter and tea, Nellie,' Mrs Kincaid ordered, remembering the name from the last time. 'I don't take much,' she informed Blakely, 'in the middle of the day. And jam,' she called after the waitress.

'It's my main meal,' Blakely explained, a note of mild justification in his tone.

'Convenient, to go out for it.'

'Ach, it is.'

'You live in the town, Mr Blakely?'

'A bit out.'

'I thought maybe you would. You have the look of the open air.'

'I'm a turkey farmer.'

'Well, there you are.'

He worried a piece of beef into shreds, piled cabbage and potato on to his fork, soaking up a little gravy before conveying the lot to his mouth.

'Not bad,' he responded when he was asked if turkeys were fetching well.

'Time was when turkeys were a Christmas trade and no more. Amn't I right? Not that I know a thing about poultry.'

'Oh, you're right enough.'

'I like the brown of a turkey. I'm told that's unusual.'

'It's all white flesh they go for those times.'

'You'd supply the supermarkets, would you?'

'The most of it goes that way all right. Though there's a few outlets locally.'

'I have a room above Beatty's.'

'I sell to Beatty for Christmas.'

'Well, there's a coincidence for you!'

'He's a decent man, Henry Beatty.'

'It's not a bad little room.'

Further details were exchanged – about the room and then about the rearing, slaughtering and plucking of turkeys, the European regulations there were as regards hygiene and refrigeration. Divulging that she was a Belfast woman, Mrs Kincaid talked about the city. Blakely said he hadn't been there since he lost his wife. She used to go for the shopping, he said. Brand's, he said.

'Oh, a great store, was Brand's. You were always on the farm, Mr Blakely?'

'Aye, I was.'

'I was sorry to hear there about your wife.'

'Aye.'

The plate of bread and butter arrived, with tea, and a small glass dish of gooseberry jam.

'I'm a widow myself,' Mrs Kincaid said.

'Ah, well –'

'I know, I know.'

That comment, spoken in a whisper, contrived to make

one of the two widowings, contrived to isolate with quiet poignancy a common ground. There was for an instant the feeling at the table that death had struck almost simultaneously. This feeling, for Mrs Kincaid, was a theatrical effect, since in her case no death, no widowing, had occurred. For Blakely, it was real. He finished the food he had been brought. Jelly with sponge-cake in it was placed before him, with a pot of tea.

'Are you far out of the town?' Mrs Kincaid asked.

'Ah, no. Not far.'

'I sometimes come to a quiet town for a rest. A resort most times. But this time of year they're lonely enough yet.'

'They would be surely.'

Shortly after that Blakely folded his newspaper into the side pocket of his jacket. He picked up his cap from the knob at the top of his chair. He said good-bye to Mrs Kincaid and went to pay his bill at the counter.

'Who is she, that woman?' Mrs Hirrell asked him in a whisper, and he said that Mrs Kincaid was lodging above Beatty's butcher's shop. He didn't know her name, he said, a Belfast woman in the town for a rest.

*

After that, Blakely found himself running into Mrs Kincaid quite often. She sat at his table in Hirrell's Café even when on one occasion there was an empty table just inside the door. She was in Blundell's News and Confectionery when he went in for his paper one day. Another time she was a mile out on the road when he was driving back to the farm and he waved at her and she waved back. A few days later she was there again with an umbrella up and he stopped, feeling he should offer her a lift.

'Well, now, that's very nice of you,' she said.

'Where're you heading?'

Mrs Kincaid said nowhere in particular. Just a daunder, she said, to fill in the afternoon. 'My name's Mrs Kincaid,' she added, since this information had not been given before, and went on to enquire if he ever felt that afternoons hung heavy.

Blakely replied that any hour of the day was the same to him. He tried to sound polite, picking out the right words, not wishing to seem brusque. 'That's Madole's,' he said as they passed a field with the gate wide open. Spring ploughing was in progress, Madole's man, Quin, on the tractor. Madole had a lot of land, Blakely explained, some of it stretching right back to the town's outskirts.

'Here's my own few acres,' he said when his pink-washed roadside farmhouse and turkey sheds came into view. 'Would I drop you? I'd say the rain's stopped.' Specks had come on to the windscreen after he'd turned off the wipers five minutes ago, but already they were drying away. There used to be a Kincaid in Lower Bridge Street one time, a dentist, before the present man came.

'It'll be a nice walk back,' she said, getting out of the car when Blakely drew it up before turning into his yard. She thanked him. 'What's on ahead, though?'

'Loughdoon. Three-quarters of a mile.'

'I'll take a look at it.'

'It's only small.'

'I like a small place.'

The Lacky sisters – twins of forty-five – were in the plucking shed, with the birds that were ready strung up along a rafter. The sisters were in their similar black and grey overalls, their similarly crowded teeth hugely exposed as soon as their employer entered the shed, their reddish hair bulging out of the cloth caps they wore. They had been plucking Blakely's turkeys for him for twenty-nine years, since their childhood. Quin came over when Madole gave him his time off, to help around the place in any way that was necessary.

Blakely nodded at the two women. They'd done well. He counted the prepared turkeys, sixteen of them. Two dozen were to be ready for the carrier when he called at four and they'd easily make that. The Lacky sisters threw back their heads and acknowledged his compliment by laughing shrilly. They couldn't have seen the woman he'd given a lift to, they wouldn't have heard the voices. People would be talking in Hirrel's about the way she always sat at his table, but what could he do about it? And he couldn't have passed her by on the road with rain falling. He put the car away in the lean-to and set off to repair a fence that had been in need of attention for a long while. His two sheepdogs went with him, loping along at his heels.

The job took longer than he'd estimated. By the time he'd finished it the carrier had been and the Lackys had gone home. The dogs began to bark when he was mixing the evening feed.

'Now that's for you,' Mrs Kincaid said, holding out something in a brown-paper bag. It was raining lightly, but she'd taken her umbrella down. 'I sheltered in Mullin's,' she said. 'That's a comfy wee bar he has there.'

Blakely stared at the bag she held out to him. 'What is it?' he said.

She smiled, shaking her head to indicate he'd have to find out himself. 'Cheer you up, Mr Blakely.'

He didn't want to accept a present from her. There was no call for her to give him a present. There was no call for her to come into the yard, looking for him.

'No need,' he said, taking a bottle of Bushmills whiskey from the damp paper bag. 'No,' he protested. The two sheepdogs, which he had pointed into a corner, had begun to creep forward on their haunches. 'Ah, no,' he said, handing back the bottle and the bag. 'Ah no, no.'

The rain was getting heavier. 'Would you mind if I stood in your turf shed for a minute?' she said. 'You get on with your work, Mr Blakely. The little offering's for your kindness, letting me share your table and that. Mullin said you took a glass like the next man.'

'I can't take this from you.'

'It's nothing, Mr Blakely.'

'Come into the kitchen till it clears.'

She said she didn't want to interrupt him, but he led the way into the house, not saying anything himself. In the kitchen he pulled the damper out on the Rayburn to warm the place up. The bottle and the bag were on the table.

'You're looking frozen, Mr Blakely,' she said, surprising him by taking two glasses from the dresser. She opened the bottle and poured whiskey for both of them. It was nothing, she said again.

It wasn't an evening when Quin came, which Blakely was glad about. The Lackys couldn't have missed her on the road, but they wouldn't have known who she was and they'd never have guessed she'd turn in to the yard.

'He told me about you,' she was saying now. 'Mr Mullin did.'

'I go in there the odd time.'

'He told me about the loss of your wife. How it was. And your daughter, of course.'

Blakely didn't say anything. The whiskey was warm in his chest. In spite of what Mullin had said he wasn't a drinking man, but he appreciated a drop of Bushmills. A going-away present, she said.

'You're going back soon?' he asked, not pressing the question, keeping it casual.

She had taken her coat off. She was wearing a blue dress with tiny flashes of red in it, like pencil dots. There was a scarf, entirely red, tucked in at the top. At the table one leg was crossed over the other, both knees shiny because the stocking material was taut. Her umbrella was cocked up on the flags to dry.

'Sooner or later,' she said. 'Cheers!'

She added more to both their glasses when he'd taken another mouthful. She looked round the kitchen and said it was lovely. 'Mabel,' she said.

'What?'

'Mabel Kincaid.'

The rain was heavy now, rattling on the window panes. The Rayburn had begun to roar. He got up to push the damper in a bit.

'That's the mother and father of a shower,' she said.

'Yes.'

'You never smile, Mr Blakely.'

Blakely was embarrassed by that. 'I think maybe I'm a dour kind of man.'

'You're not at all. But after what I heard I wouldn't blame you.'

She asked if he had always lived in this house, and he said he had. His father bought the few fields from Madole, farming pigs in those days. It was the Madoles who'd built the house and they'd built it without foundations, which his father didn't know until after he'd bought it, didn't know that was why he'd got it cheap.

'A big family was it, Mr Blakely?'

He shook his head. A family of four, he said, one more than his own family, later on. 'I have a brother, Willie John.'

As soon as he mentioned Willie John's name Willie John laughed silently in Blakely's recall, his big jaw split, the freckles around his eyes merging as the flesh puckered. Huge and ungainly, ham-fisted their father called him before the first fruits of those same hands were completed – a twin-engined Dewoitine 510, built from a kit.

'We used to fly them out in the fields.' He didn't know why he told her; he hadn't meant to, but sometimes, with whiskey, he was garrulous, even though he still hadn't drunk much. Drink had a way of bringing things to life for him and he felt it doing that now. A Messerschmitt came to rest in a clump of nettles and Willie John gingerly rescued it, noting the damage to the tail-piece and one of the wings. His own Black Widow took off, airborne until the lighter fuel in the engine ran out. It glided down on to the cropped grass. Bloody marvellous, Willie John said.

'Just the two of you,' she said. 'I was an only myself.'

'Willie John got out when the troubles began. I get a card, Christmas time. Denver, Colorado.'

The telephone rang in the hall. It was Nathan Smith from Ulsterfare with the order for next week. When they finished talking about the turkeys Nathan said his daughter had got herself engaged.

'I heard it. Isn't that great, Nathan?'

'It is surely. All we need now is the quiet'll last for the wedding. Thursday will we say for the order?'

'No problem, Nathan.'

In the kitchen she was on her feet with the frying-pan in her hand. The frying-pan had the breakfast fat congealed on it. She'd taken rashers out of the fridge and had lifted up one of the covers of the Rayburn. There were knives and forks on the table.

'I was hoping you'd be longer,' she said. 'I had a surprise planned.'

'Oh, look –'

'Sit down and take another drop. It's still at it cats and dogs. You have sausages in there. Would you take a couple?'

'The rain's no worry. I can run you back.'

She shook her head. She'd never ask a man who'd been

drinking to drive. She spread four rashers on the fat of the pan and put the pan on the heat. She pricked four sausages on the draining-board. 'Have you eggs?' she said.

He brought in a bowl of eggs from the scullery. A woman hadn't cooked in the kitchen since Hetty and Jacqueline died. He couldn't remember that a woman had even been in the house since the last of the funeral guests stepped out of it, certainly not the Lackys. He shouldn't have talked about Willie John like that. Talk had encouraged her. He shouldn't have taken the Bushmills.

'When it clears up I'll walk it,' she said. 'I'm only filling in the time, Mr Blakely.'

'I'll drive you in,' he insisted. 'I'm well known. They won't stop me.'

*

Mrs Kincaid undressed herself, thinking about him. He was a finished man. The man in the bar had said as much. He'd been destroyed by the troubles, but even so he kept going, with his turkeys and the two queer-looking women she'd met on the road working for him, feathers all over their overalls. His dinner every day in a café that overcharged you, his memories of toy aeroplanes, the wife and daughter never talked about: that was it for him. A Christmas card from Denver kept his spirits up.

Removing the last of her underclothes, Mrs Kincaid guessed that he was thinking about her also, that he might even be seeing her as she was in this very minute. Finished or not, there was always a spark that could be kindled. An old hand at that, Mrs Kincaid didn't have to ask herself whether or not, today, she had done so. She had broken her resolve and she wondered as she buttoned her nightdress if she had the will to draw back now, to move on tomorrow, before things went any further. She lay for a moment with the bedside light on, then reached out and turned it off. She felt as she had often felt when she got to this stage in a bit of business – that some shadow of herself was having its way with her, that if eighty-four thousand pounds hadn't been lifted off her she'd be a different woman entirely.

'Left high and dry,' she murmured in the darkness, applying the expression to the turkey farmer, dozily remembering that it was the one she had used about herself when she'd suffered her calamity.

*

On the morning after the evening of Mrs Kincaid's visit to his house Blakely was aware of not minding if people had seen her in his car when he'd driven her to her room above Beatty's shop. Her company in his kitchen had not, in the end, been disagreeable. She had washed up the dishes from which they had eaten the food she'd cooked. She had been sympathetic about several matters, and before they left he had shown her the plucking and dressing sheds even though he'd told himself he shouldn't. 'Isn't it lonely for you?' she'd said.

She wasn't in Hirrel's that day, nor the next. She'll have gone, Blakely thought. She had bought him the bottle and now she'd gone back to Belfast. He hadn't been welcoming;

he'd been cagey and suspicious, worried in case the Lackys knew she'd cooked his food, worried in case Quin walked in. He was thinking about her when he heard the dogs barking and her voice quietening them.

'I was passing by,' she said.

The friendship that began for Blakely when the Bushmills was poured again and when for the second time a meal was shared in his kitchen was later remarked upon in Hirrel's and in the turkey sheds. Because of his trouble in the past people were pleased, and pleased again when the two were seen together on the steps of the Stella Four-Screen. Reports went round that they'd danced, one Friday night, in the Crest Ballroom; a corner of the bar in Digby's Hotel became known as theirs.

Soon after that the Lackys met Mrs Kincaid, and Quin did. She was brought to Sunday lunch with the Reverend Johnston. One morning Blakely woke up aware of a deep longing for Mrs Kincaid, aware of a gentleness when he thought about her, of an impatience with himself for not declaring his feelings before this.

*

'Oh no, dear, no.'

She said he was too good for her. Too good a man, she said, too steady a man, too well-set-up, too decent a man. She could bring nothing, she said, she would be coming empty-handed and that was never her way. Kincaid had left her no more than a pittance, she said, not expecting to be taken so soon, as no man would in the prime of his life. A few years ago Mrs Kincaid had heard talk of a Belfast man who'd electrocuted himself drilling holes in an outside wall: as the cause of Kincaid's demise, that did well enough.

'No, I never could,' she repeated, surveying the astonishment she had known would appear in the lean features, the flush of the cheeks darkening. 'You have your life the way it is,' she said. 'You have your memories. I'd never upset the way things are with you.'

He went silent. Was he thinking he'd made a fool of himself? she wondered. Would he finish his drink and that would be the end of it?

'I'm on my own,' he said.

They were in the bar of the hotel, the quiet time between six and seven. The day before she'd said she'd definitely be off at the end of the week. Refreshed and invigorated, she'd said.

'I'm alone,' he repeated.

'Don't I know you are? Didn't I say you'd be lonely?'

'What I'm saying to you –'

'I know what you're saying to me. What I'm saying to yourself is you're set in your ways. You're well-to-do, I haven't much. Isn't it about that too?'

'It's not money –'

'There's always money.'

The conversation softly became argument. Affection spread through it, real and contrived. It had been great knowing him, Mrs Kincaid said. You come to a place, you gain a friend; nothing was nicer. But Blakely was stubborn. There were feelings in this, he insisted; she couldn't deny it.

'I'm not. I'm not at all. I'm only trying to be fair to you. I have a Belfast woman's caution in me.'

'I'm as cautious myself as any man in Ulster. I have a name for it.'

'You're trusting the unknown all the same. Fair and square, hasn't that to be said?'

'You're never unknown to me.'

'When the cards are down I'm a woman you don't know from a tinker.'

Blakely denied that with a gesture. He didn't say anything. Mrs Kincaid said:

'If I asked you for money, why would you give it to me? I wouldn't do it, but if I did. Who'd blame you for shaking your head? If I said write me a cheque for two thousand pounds who'd blame you for saying no? No man in his senses would say anything else. If I said to you I'd keep that cheque by me, that I'd never pass it into the bank because it was only there as a bond of trust between us, you wouldn't believe me.'

'Why wouldn't I trust you?'

'That's what I'm saying to you. I'm a woman turned up in the town to get away for a little while from the noise and bustle of the city. Who'd blame you if you'd say to yourself I wouldn't trust her as far as an inch? When there's trust between us, is what I'm saying, we'll maybe talk about the other. D'you understand me, dear?'

'We know each other well.'

'We do and we don't, dear. Bad things have happened to us.'

Mrs Kincaid spoke then of the trouble in her past, speaking only the truth, as always she did at this stage in the proceedings.

*

Blakely felt in the inside pocket of his jacket and took out a Northern Bank cheque-book. He wrote the cheque. He dated it and signed it and tore it out. He handed it to her. She took it, staring at it for as long as a minute. Then she tore it up.

'Please,' he said. 'I mean it.'

'I never knew a straighter man,' Mrs Kincaid said, and for a moment longer the open cheque-book lay between them on the bar-room table. When he reached for it again she said, 'I bank under my maiden name.' She gave him a name, which he added to the *Mabel* he had written while she was speaking. 'That will never be cashed,' she said. 'I promise you that.'

They would not correspond, she laid down. They would wait two months and then they would meet again at the table they were at now, the table they had made their own. They chose a date and a time, a Tuesday at the end of July.

*

The cheque was for the amount Mrs Kincaid had mentioned. She paid it into her bank as soon as she was back in Belfast and recorded the amount in her notebook. Two days later it reached Blakely's bank and was covered by his standing instruction that if his current account ever did not have sufficient funds in it a transfer should be made from his deposit account. He received his next bank statement sixteen days later.

*

She could have married the man. The clergyman she'd been introduced to would have done the job. She could have been the wife of a turkey farmer for the rest of her days and she wondered about that – about waking in the farmhouse and the sheepdogs in the yard, about conversations there might have been, their common ground as the victims of gangsters.

Regret nagged Mrs Kincaid then. She felt she had missed a chance she hadn't even known was there. Her instinct was to write a letter, although what she might say in it she didn't know. The more she wondered if she should or not, the more her confidence grew that inspiration would come to her, that in the end she would fill a page or two as easily as she made an entry in her notebook. Time would pass, and she had faith in the way time had of softening anything which was distressful. Naturally the poor man would have been distressed.

*

Sadness afflicted Blakely, which eased a little while that time went by. Resignation took its place. It was his fault; he had been foolish. His resistance had been there, he had let it slip away. But even so, on the day they had arranged to meet, he put on his suit and went along to Digby's Hotel.

He waited for an hour in their corner of the bar, believing

that against the odds there might somehow be an explanation. Then he went away.

Somewhere in him as he drove out of the town there was still a flicker of optimism, although he did not know where it came from or even if what it promised was sensible. He did not dwell upon his mood; it was simply there.

*

The troubles had returned since Mrs Kincaid had travelled back to Belfast. There had been murder and punishment, the burning of churches, the barricades at Drumcree, the destruction of the town of Omagh. Yet belief in the fragile peace persisted, too precious after so long to abandon. Stubbornly the people of the troubles honoured the hope that had spread among them, fierce in their clamour that it should not go away. In spite of the quiet made noisy again, its benign infection had reached out for Blakely; it did so for Mrs Kincaid also, even though her trouble was her own. Weary at last of making entries in a notebook, she wrote her letter.

The Telephone Game

Since the conventional separation of the sexes on the evening before a wedding did not appeal to Liese, Tony agreed that there should be a party to which both sides of the wedding came instead. A party was necessary because the formalities of the day would not allow for much of a reunion with friends they had not seen for some time, but they did not wish the reception to be an occasion that went on and on in order to cater for this: they wanted to be in Venice in time for the first dinner of their marriage. So in Tony's flat, already re-arranged for married life, his friends and Liese's mixed jollily in advance, while wine flowed generously and there was background music that was danced to, while tomorrow's bride and groom learnt a little more about one another from what was said. Friendships here were longer than their own.

Tonight, there was a solemnity about Liese's manner that softened further the beauty of her features: her mind was on her marriage. Smooth, pale as wheat, her hair fell to her shoulders; her light-blue eyes were a degree less tranquil than usually they were, but when she smiled all that tranquillity came back. 'Oh, Tony, you are lucky,' a cousin who had not met Liese before remarked, and Tony said he knew it. He was fair-haired too, by nature insouciant and humorous, handsome in his way.

In Germany Liese's father was a manufacturer of gloves. In England Tony had been looked after by an aunt ever since his parents died in the worst air disaster of 1977 – the runway collision of two jumbo-jets – when Tony was six, an only child. Nineteen years later he and Liese had met by chance, in a bustling lunchtime restaurant, not far from Victoria Station. 'D'you think we could meet again?' he had pleaded, while a tubby, middle-aged waitress, bringing their coffee in that moment, approved of his boldness and let it show. 00178 was the number on the back of the driver's seat in the first taxi they sat in together, black digits on an oval of white enamel. Afterwards, romantically, they both remembered that, and the taxi-driver's conversation, and the tubby waitress.

Already in love, Liese had heard about the tragedy in 1977, Tony about the gloves that had been the source of livelihood in Liese's family for generations, lambskin and pigskin, goatskin and doeskin. Hand-stitching and dyeing skills, a different way with gussets for the different leathers, were talked about when for the first time Tony visited Schelesnau, when he was shown the long rows of templates and the contented workforce, the knives and thonging tools tidily on their racks. In Schelesnau, driven by love, he played the part required of him, asking questions and showing an interest. Liese was nervous in anticipation before meeting Tony's aunt, who was getting on a bit now in a small South Coast resort with a distant view of the ferries plying back and forth to France. But Liese needn't have been apprehensive. 'She's lovely,'

Tony's aunt said, and in Schelesnau – where there were Liese's two younger sisters and a busy family life – Tony was considered charming. There was at first – in Schelesnau and in England – a faint concern that the marriage was taking on a burden that marriage did not always have to, that would have been avoided if Liese had chosen to marry a German or Tony an English girl: after all, there had been enmity in two terrible wars. It was a vague feeling, very much at odds with the sentiments of the time, and although it hovered like some old, long-discredited ghost, it failed in the end to gain a place in the scheme of things. What did, instead, was the telephone game.

On the night before the wedding it was Tony who suggested playing it. Afterwards, he hardly knew why he did, why he had imagined that Germans would understand the humour of the game, but of course he'd had a certain amount to drink. For her part, Liese wished she had insisted that her wedding party wasn't an occasion for this kind of diversion. 'Oh, Tony!' was her single, half-hearted protest, and Tony didn't hear it.

Already he had explained to Liese's sisters – both of whom were to be bridesmaids – that strangers were telephoned, that you won if you held a stranger in conversation longer than anyone else could. The information was passed around the bewildered Germans, who politely wondered what was coming next.

'I am in engine boats,' a man who had been a classmate of Liese's in Fräulein Groenewold's kindergarten was saying when the music was turned off. 'Outboards, you say?'

He, and all the others – more than thirty still left at the party – were asked to be silent then. A number was dialled by Tony's best man and the first of the strangers informed that there was a gas leak in the street, asked to check the rooms of his house for a tell-tale smell, then to return to the phone with information as to that. The next was told that an external fuse had blown, that all electrical connections should be unplugged or turned off to obviate danger. The next was advised to close and lock his windows against a roving polecat.

'The Water Board here,' Tony said when his turn came. 'We're extremely sorry to ring you so late. We have an emergency.'

Some of the German visitors were still perplexed. 'So they are all your friends?' a girl with a plait asked, in spite of what had been said. 'This is a joke with friends?'

Liese explained again that the people who were telephoned were just anyone. The game was to delay, to keep a conversation going. She whispered, in case her voice should carry to Tony's victim. '*Was? Stimmt irgendwas nicht?*' her friend whispered back, and Liese said it was all just for fun. The last call had lasted three and three-quarter minutes, the one before only a few seconds.

'What we would like you to do,' Tony said, 'is to make your way to the water tanks in your loft and turn off the inlet tap. This tap is usually red, madam, but of course the colour may have worn off. What we're endeavouring to do is to prevent the flooding of your house.'

'Flooding?' the woman he spoke to repeated, her voice drowsy with sleep. 'Eh?'

'One of our transformer valves has failed. We have a dangerously high pressure level.'

'I can't go up into the loft at this hour. It's the middle of the night.'

'We're having to ask everyone in the area, madam. Perhaps your husband –'

'I ain't got no husband. I ain't got no one here. I'm seventy-three years of age. How d'you think I'd know about a tap?'

'We're sorry for the inconvenience, madam. We naturally would not ask you to do this if it were not necessary. When a transformer valve goes it is a vital matter. The main articulated valve may go next and then of course it is too late. When the articulated valve goes the flood-water could rise to sixteen feet within minutes. In which case I would advise you to keep to the upstairs rooms.'

Tony put the palm of his hand over the mouthpiece. She had beetled off to get a stepladder, he whispered, and a flashlight. He listened again and said there was the mewing of a cat.

'It'll be all right now?' another German girl leaned forward to ask Liese, and the German who was in outboard engines, who perfectly understood the game, gestured with a smile that it would be. The game was amusing, he considered, but not a game to play in Schelesnau. It was sophisticated. It was the famous English sense of humour.

Tony heard the shuffle of footsteps, a door closing in the distance, and in the distance also the mewing of the cat again. Then there was silence.

Tony looked round his guests, some of them, as he was, a little drunk. He laughed, careless now of allowing the sound to pass to the other house, since its lone occupant was presumably already in her loft. He put the receiver down beside the directories on the narrow telephone table, and reached out with a bottle of Sancerre to attend to a couple of empty glasses. A friend he'd been at school with began to tell of an occasion when a man in Hoxton was sent out on to the streets to see if a stolen blue van had just been parked there. He himself had once posed as the proprietor of a ballroom-dancing school, offering six free lessons. Some of the Germans said they must be going now.

'Shh.' Listening again, Tony held up a hand. But there was no sound from the other end. 'She's still aloft,' he said, and put the receiver down beside the directories.

'Where're you staying?' the best man asked, his lips brushing the cheek of the girl with the plait as they danced, the music there again. The telephone game had run its course.

'In Germany,' it was explained by the man in outboard motors, 'we might say this was *Ärgernis*.'

'Oh, here too,' an English girl who did not approve of the telephone game said. 'If that means harassment.'

Those who remained left in a bunch then, the Germans telling about *Wasservexierungsport*, a practical joke involving jets of water. You put your ten pfennigs into a slot machine to bring the lights on in a grotto and found yourself drenched instead. 'Water-vexing,' the outboard-motors man translated.

*

'You could stay here, you know,' Tony said when he and Liese had collected the glasses and the ashtrays, when everything had been washed and dried, the cushions plumped up, a window opened to let in a stream of cold night air.

'But I have yet to finish packing up my things. The morning will be busy.'

They walked about the flat that soon would be their home, going from room to room, although they knew the rooms well. Softly, the music still played, and they danced a little in the small hall, happy to be alone now. The day they'd met there had been an office party in the busy lunchtime restaurant, a lot of noise, and a woman in a spotted red dress quarrelling with her friend at the table next to theirs. How cautious Liese had been that day was afterwards remembered, and how cautious she'd been – much later – when Tony said he loved her. Remembered, too, with that same fondness was how both of them had wanted marriage, not some substitute, how they had wanted the binding of its demands and vows and rigours. London was the city of their romance and it was in London – to the discomfort and annoyance of her parents, defying all convention – that Liese had insisted the marriage should take place.

While they danced, Tony noticed that his telephone receiver was still lying beside the directories. More than half an hour ago he had forgotten about it. He reached to pick it up, bringing their dance to an end. He said:

'She hasn't put hers back.'

Liese took the receiver from him. She listened, too, and

heard the empty sound of a connected line. 'Hullo,' she said. 'Hullo.'

'She forgot. She went to bed.'

'Would she forget, Tony?'

'Well, something like it.'

'She give a name? You have the number still?'

Tony shook his head. 'She didn't give a name.' He had forgotten the number; he'd probably never even been aware of it, he said.

'What did she say, Tony?'

'Only that she was without a husband.'

'Her husband was out? At this time?'

They had drawn away from one another. Tony turned the music off. He said:

'She meant she was widowed. She wasn't young. Seventy-three or something like that.'

'This old woman goes to her loft –'

'Well, I mean, she said she would. More likely, she didn't believe a word I said.'

'She went to look for a stepladder and a flashlight. You told us.'

'I think she said she was cold in her nightdress. More likely, she just went back to bed. I don't blame her.'

Listening again, Liese said:

'I can hear the cat.'

But when she passed the receiver over, Tony said he couldn't hear anything. Nothing whatsoever, he said.

'Very far away. The cat was mewing, and suddenly it stopped. Don't put it back!' Liese cried when Tony was about to return the receiver to its cradle. 'She is there in her loft, Tony.'

'Oh, honestly, I don't think so. Why should she be? It doesn't take long to turn a stop-cock off.'

'What is a stop-cock?'

'Just a way of controlling the water.'

The mewing of the cat came faintly to him, a single mew and then another. Not knowing why he did so, Tony shook his head again, silently denying this sound. Liese said:

'She could have fallen down. It would be hard to see with her flashlight and she could have fallen down.'

'No, I don't think so.' For the first time in the year and a half she had known him Liese heard a testiness in Tony's voice. There was no point in not replacing the receiver, he said. 'Look, let's forget it, Liese.'

Solemnly, but in distress, Liese gazed into the features of the man she was to marry in just over twelve hours' time. He smiled a familiar, easy smile. No point, he said again, more softly. No point of any kind in going on about this.

'Honestly, Liese.'

They had walked about, that first afternoon. He had taken her through Green Park, then down to the river. She was in London to perfect her English; that afternoon she should have been at another class. And it was a quarter past five before Tony explained, untruthfully, his absence from his desk. The next day they met again.

'Nothing has happened, Liese.'

'She could be dead.'

'Oh, Liese, don't be silly.'

At once, having said that, Tony apologized. Of course she wasn't silly. That game was silly. He was sorry they'd played it tonight.

'But, Tony –'

'Of course she isn't dead.'

'Why do you think you can be sure?'

He shook his head, meaning to indicate that he wasn't claiming to be sure, only that reason implied what he suggested. During the months they were getting to know one another he had learnt that Liese's imagination was sometimes a nuisance; she had said so herself. Purposeless and dispensable, she said, a quirk of nature that caused her, too often, to doubt the surface of things. Music was purposeless, he had replied, the petal of a flower dispensable: what failed the market-place was often what should be treasured most. But Liese called her quirk of nature a pest; and experiencing an instance of it for the first time now, Tony understood.

'Let's not quarrel, Liese.'

But the quarrel – begun already while neither noticed – spread, insidious in the stillness that the silent telephone, once more passed from hand to hand, seemed to inspire. Neither heard the mewing of the cat again, and Tony said:

'Look, in the morning she'll see that receiver hanging there and she'll remember she forgot to put it back.'

'It is morning now. Tony, we could go to the police.'

'The *police*? What on earth for?'

'They could find out where that house is.'

'Oh, none of this makes sense!' And Tony, who happened

just then to be holding the telephone receiver, would again have replaced it.

Liese snatched it, anger flushing through her cheeks. She asked him why he'd wanted to do that, and he shrugged and didn't answer. He didn't because all this was ridiculous, because he didn't trust himself to say anything.

'The police couldn't find out,' he said after a silence had gone on. The police wouldn't have a telephone number to go on. All they could tell the police was that in a house somewhere in London there was an old woman and a cat. All over London, Tony said, there were old women and cats.

'Tony, try to remember the number.'

'Oh, for God's sake! How can I remember the bloody number when I didn't even know it in the first place?'

'Well, then it will be in the computers.'

'What computers?'

'In Germany all calls go into the computers.'

Liese didn't know if this was so or not. What she knew was that they could do nothing if he had put the receiver back. Why had he wanted to?

'Darling, we can't,' he was saying now. 'We can't just walk round to a police station at nearly three o'clock in the morning to report that an old woman has gone up to her loft. It was a harmless game, Liese.'

She tried to say nothing, but did not succeed. The words came anyway, unchosen, ignoring her will.

'It is a horrible game. How can it not be horrible when it ends like this?'

The old woman lies there, Liese heard her own voice insist.

And light comes up through the open trapdoor, and the stepladder is below. There are the dusty boards, the water pipes. The cat's eyes are pinpricks in the gloom.

'Has she struck her head, Tony? And bones go brittle when you're old. I'm saying what could be true.'

'We have no reason whatsoever to believe any of this has happened.'

'The telephone left hanging –'

'She did not replace the telephone because she forgot to.'

'You asked her to come back. You said to do what you asked and to tell you if it was done.'

'Sometimes people can tell immediately that it's a put-up thing.'

'Hullo! Hullo!' Liese agitatedly shouted into the receiver. 'Hullo . . . Please.'

'Liese, we have to wait until she wakes up again.'

'At least the cat will keep the mice away.'

Other people will see the lights left on. Other people will come to the house and find the dangling telephone. Why should an old woman in her night clothes set a stepladder under a trapdoor? The people who come will ask that. They'll give the cat a plate of milk and then they'll put the telephone back, and one of them will climb up the ladder.

'I wish it had happened some other night.'

'Liese –'

'You wanted to put the receiver back. You wanted not to know. You wanted us for ever not to know, to make a darkness of it.'

'No, of course I didn't.'

'Sometimes a person doesn't realize. A person acts in some way and doesn't realize.'

'Please,' Tony begged again and Liese felt his arms around her. Tears for a moment smudged away the room they were in, softly he stroked her hair. When she could speak she whispered through his murmured consolation, repeating that she wished all this had happened sooner, not tonight. As though some illness had struck her, she experienced a throbbing ache, somewhere in her body, she didn't know where. That came from muddle and confusion was what she thought, or else from being torn apart, as if she possessed two selves. There was not room for quarrels between them. There had not been, there was not still. Why had it happened tonight, why now? Like a hammering in Liese's brain, this repetition went on, began again as a persistent roundabout. Imagining was Gothic castles and her own fairytales made up when she was in Fräulein Groenewold's kindergarten, and fantasies with favourite film stars later on. It became a silliness when reality was distorted. Of course he was right.

'I can't help thinking of her,' Liese whispered none the less. 'I cannot help it.'

Tony turned away, and slowly crossed to the window. He wanted to be outside, to walk about the streets, to have a chance to think. He had been asked to reason with Liese when she wanted her wedding to be in London. A longish letter had come from Schelesnau, pleading with him to intervene, to make her see sense. It was inconvenient for everyone; it was an added and unnecessary expense; it was *exzentrisch* of her.

Tonight Liese had learnt that Tony had been daring as a boy, that he had walked along a ledge from one dormitory window to another, eighteen feet above the ground. She had delighted in that – that he had not told her himself, that he was courageous and did not boast of it. Yet everything seemed different now.

'It is a feeling,' Liese said.

At the window, Tony stared down into the empty street. The artificial light had not yet been extinguished and would not be for hours. Yet dawn had already crept in, among the parked cars, the plastic sacks brought up from basements the night before, bicycles chained to railings. What did she mean, a feeling?

'Honestly, there is no reason to be upset.'

As he spoke, Tony turned from the window. Liese's face was tight and nervous now, for a moment not beautiful. The air that came into the room was refreshingly cold, and again he wanted to be walking in it, alone somewhere. She did not love him was what she meant, she had been taken from him. He said so, staring down into the street again, his back to her.

'Oh no, I love you, Tony.'

All over London, sleeping now, were tomorrow's wedding guests – her mother and her father, her friends come all the way from Schelesnau. Her sisters' bridesmaids' dresses were laid out. Flowers had been ordered, and a be-ribboned car. The grass of the hotel lawns was trimmed for the reception. In her house by the sea Tony's aunt had ironed the clothes she'd chosen, and Liese imagined them waiting on their hangers. The morning flights would bring more guests from Germany. She had been stubborn about the city of their romance. There would have been no old woman's sleep disturbed in Schelesnau, no ugly unintended incident. Why did she know that the dead were carried from a house in a plain long box, not a coffin?

'We are different kinds of people, Tony.'

'Because you are German and I am English? Is that it? That history means something after all?'

She shook her head. Why did he think that? Why did he go off so much in the wrong direction, seizing so readily a useful cliché?

'We are not enemies, we are friends.' She said a little more, trying to explain what did not seem to her to be complicated. Yet she felt she made it so, for the response was bewilderment.

'Remember that office party?' Tony said. 'The quarrelling woman in red? The waitress smiling when we went off together? 00178. Remember that?'

She tried to, but the images would not come as clearly as they usually did. 'Yes, I remember,' she said.

The doubt in their exchanges brought hesitation, was an inflexion that could not be disguised. Silences came, chasms that each time were wider.

'This has to do with us, not with the past we did not know.' Liese shook her head, firm in her emphasis.

Tony nodded and, saying nothing, felt the weight of patience. He wondered about it in a silence that went on for minutes, before there was the far-off rattle of the human voice, faint and small. He looked from the window to where

Liese had laid the receiver on the table. He watched her move to pick it up.

*

They stood together while a clergyman repeated familiar lines. A ring was passed from palm to palm. When the last words were spoken they turned to walk away together from the clergyman and the altar.

The wedding guests strolled on tidy hotel lawns. A photographer fussed beneath a bright blue sky. 'You are more beautiful than I ever knew,' Tony whispered while more champagne was drunk and there was talk in German and in English. 'And I love you more.'

Liese smiled in the moment they had purloined, before another speech was called for, before her father expressed his particular joy that the union of two families brought with it today the union of two nations. 'We are two foolish people,' Tony had said when at last the telephone receiver was replaced, after the journey to the loft had been retailed in detail, an apology offered because carrying out the instructions had taken so long. They had embraced, the warmth of their relief sensual as they clung to one another. And the shadow of truth that had come was lost in the euphoria.

'I'm sorry,' Liese said in the next day's sunshine. 'I'm sorry I was a nuisance.'

Glasses were raised to greater happiness than the happiness of the day. Together they smiled and waved from the car when it came to take them away. Then private at last, they let their tiredness show, each reaching for a hand. Their thoughts were different. He had been right. Yet again, for Tony, that conclusion repeated itself: not for an instant in the night had he doubted that he'd been right. Did love spawn victims? Liese wondered. Had they been warned off a territory of unease that did not yet seem so? Why was it that passing incidents seemed more significant in people's lives and their relationships than the enmity or amity of nations? For a moment Liese wanted to speak of that, and almost did before deciding not to.

The Hill Bachelors

In the kitchen of the farmhouse she wondered what they'd do about her, what they'd suggest. It was up to them; she couldn't ask. It wouldn't be seemly to ask, it wouldn't feel right.

She was a small woman, spare and wiry, her mourning clothes becoming her. At sixty-eight she had ailments: arthritis in her knuckles and her ankles, though only slightly a nuisance to her; a cataract she was not yet aware of. She had given birth without much difficulty to five children, and was a grandmother to nine. Born herself far from the hills that were her home now, she had come to this house forty-seven years ago, had shared its kitchen and the rearing of geese and hens with her husband's mother, until the kitchen and the rearing became entirely her own. She hadn't thought she would be left. She hadn't wanted it. She didn't now.

*

He walked into the hills from where the bus had dropped him on the main road, by Caslin's petrol pumps and shop across the road from the Master McGrath Bar and Lounge, owned by the Caslins also. It was midday and it was fine. After four hours in two different buses he welcomed the walk and the fresh air. He had dressed himself for the funeral so that he wouldn't have to bring the extra clothes in a suitcase he'd have had to borrow. Overnight necessities were in a ragged blue shopping bag which, every working day, accompanied him in the cab of the lorry he drove, delivering sacks of flour to the premises of bakers, and cartons of pre-packed bags to retailers.

Everything was familiar to him: the narrow road, in need of repair for as long as he had known it, the slope rising gently at first, the hills in the far distance becoming mountains, fields and conifers giving way to marsh and a growth that couldn't be identified from where he walked but which he knew was fern, then heather and bog cotton with here and there a patch of grass. Not far below the skyline were the corrie lakes he had never seen.

He was a dark-haired young man of twenty-nine, slightly made, pink cheeks and a certain chubbiness about his features giving him a genial, easygoing air. He was untroubled as he walked on, reflecting only that a drink and a packet of potato crisps at the Master McGrath might have been a good idea. He wondered how Maureen Caslin had turned out; when they were both fifteen he'd thought the world of her.

At a crossroads he turned to the left, on to an unmade-up boreen, scarcely more than a track. Around him there was a silence he remembered also, quite different from the kind of silence he had become used to in or around the midland towns for which, eleven years ago, he had left these hills. It was broken when he had walked another mile by no more than what seemed like a vibration in the air, a faint disturbance that might have been, at some great distance, the throb of an aeroplane. Five minutes later, rust-eaten and muddy, a front wing replaced but not yet painted, Hartigan's old red Toyota clattered over the potholes and the tractor tracks. The two men waved to each other and then the ramshackle car stopped.

'How're you, Paulie?' Hartigan said.

'I'm all right, Mr Hartigan. How're you doing yourself?'

Hartigan said he'd been better. He leaned across to open the passenger door. He said he was sorry, and Paulie knew what he meant. He had wondered if he'd be in luck, if Hartigan would be coming back from Drunbeg this midday. A small, florid man, Hartigan lived higher up in the hills with a sister who was more than a foot taller than he was, a lean, gangling woman who liked to be known only as Miss Hartigan. On the boreen there were no other houses.

'They'll be coming back?' Hartigan enquired above the rasping noise of the Toyota's engine, referring to Paulie's two brothers and two sisters.

'Ah, they will surely.'

'He was out in the big field on the Tuesday.'

Paulie nodded. Hartigan drove slowly. It wasn't a time for conversation, and that was observed.

'Thanks, Mr Hartigan,' Paulie said as they parted, and waved when the Toyota drove on. The sheepdogs barked at him and he patted their heads, recognizing the older one. The yard was tidy. Hartigan hadn't said he'd been down lending a hand but Paulie could tell he had. The back door was open, his mother expecting him.

'It's good you came back,' she said.

He shook his head, realizing as soon as he had made it that the gesture was too slight for her to have noticed. He couldn't not have come back. 'How're you doing?' he said.

'All right. All right.'

They were in the kitchen. His father was upstairs. The others would come and then the coffin would be closed and his father would be taken to the church. That was how she wanted it: the way it always was when death was taken from the house.

'It was never good between you,' she said.

'I'd come all the same.'

Nothing was different in the kitchen: the same green paint, worn away to the timber at two corners of the dresser and around the latch of the doors that led to the yard and to the stairs; the same delft seeming no more chipped or cracked on the dresser shelves, the big scrubbed table, the clutter on the smoky mantel-shelf above the stove, the uncomfortable chairs, the flagged floor, the receipts on the spike in the window.

'Sit with him a while, Paulie.'

His father had always called him Paul, and he was called Paul in his employment, among the people of the midland towns. Paul was what Patsy Finucane called him.

'Go up to him, Paulie. God rest him,' she said, a plea in her tone that bygones should be bygones, that the past should be misted away now that death had come, that prayer for the safe delivery of a soul was what mattered more.

'Will they all come together?' he asked, still sitting there. 'Did they say that?'

'They'll be here by three. Kevin's car and one Aidan'll hire.'

He stood up, his chair scraping on the flagstones. He had asked the questions in order to delay going up to his father's bedside. But it was what she wanted, and what she was saying without saying it was that it was what his father wanted also. There would be forgiveness in the bedroom, his own spoken in a mumble, his father's taken for granted.

He took the rosary she held out to him, not wishing to cause offence.

*

Hearing his footsteps on the brief, steeply pitched stairs, hearing the bedroom door open and close, the footsteps again in the room above her, then silence, she saw now what her returned son saw: the bloodless pallor, the stubble that had come, eyelids drawn, lips set, the grey hair she had combed. Frances had been the favourite, then Mena; Kevin was approved of because he was reliable; Aidan was the first-born. Paulie hadn't been often mentioned.

There was the sound of a car, far back on the boreen. A while it would take to arrive at the farmhouse. She set out cups and saucers on the table, not hurrying. The kettle had boiled earlier and she pushed it back on to the hot plate of the stove. Not since they were children had they all been back at the same time. There wouldn't be room for them for the two nights they'd have to spend, but they'd have their own ideas about how to manage that. She opened the back door so that there'd be a welcome.

*

Paulie looked down at the stretched body, not trusting himself to address it in any way. Then he heard the cars arriving and crossed the room to the window. In the yard Frances was getting out of one and the other was being backed so that it wouldn't be in the way, a white Ford he'd never seen before. The window was open at the top and he could hear the voices, Kevin saying it hadn't been a bad drive at all and Aidan agreeing. The Ford was hired, *Cahill of Limerick* it said on a sticker; picked up at Shannon it would have been.

The husbands of Paulie's sisters hadn't come, maybe because of the shortage of sleeping space. They'd be looking after the Dublin children, and it seemed that Kevin's Sharon had stayed behind with theirs in Carlow. Aidan had come on his own from Boston. Paulie had never met Aidan's wife and Sharon only once; he'd never met any of the children. They could have managed in a single car, he calculated, watching his brothers and sisters lifting out their suitcases, but it might have been difficult to organize, Kevin having to drive round by Shannon.

His brothers wore black ties, his sisters were in mourning of a kind, not entirely, because that could wait till later. Mena looked pregnant again. Kevin had a bald patch now. Aidan took off the glasses he had worn to drive. Their suitcases weren't heavy. You could tell there was no intention to stay longer than was necessary.

Looking down into the yard, Paulie knew that an assumption had already been made, as he had known it in the kitchen when he sat there with his mother. He was the bachelor of the family, the employment he had wasn't much. His mother couldn't manage on her own.

He had known it in Meagher's back bar when he told Patsy Finucane he had a funeral to go to. The death had lost him Patsy Finucane: it was her, not his father, he thought about when he heard of it, and in Meagher's the stout ran away with him and he spoke too soon. 'Jeez,' she said, 'what would I do in a farmhouse!'

*

Afterwards – when the journey through the hills had become a funeral procession at the edge of the town, when the coffin had been delivered to its night's resting place, and later when the burial was complete and the family had returned to the farmhouse and had dispersed the next morning – Paulie remained.

He had not intended to. He had hoped to get a lift in one of the two cars, and then to take a bus, and another bus, as he had on his journey over.

'Where is it they'll separate?' his mother asked in the quietness that followed the departure.

He didn't know. Somewhere that was convenient; in some town they would pull in and have a drink, different now that they weren't in a house of mourning. They would exchange news it hadn't seemed right to exchange before. Aidan would talk about Boston, offering his sisters and his brother hospitality there.

'Warm yourself at the fire, Paulie.'

'Wait till I see to the heifers first.'

'His boots are there.'

'I know.'

His brothers had borrowed the gum boots, too; wherever you went, you needed them. Kevin had fixed a fence, Aidan had got the water going again in the pipe up to the sheep. Between them, they'd taken the slack out of the barbed wire beyond the turf bog.

'Put on a waterproof, Paulie.'

It wasn't going to rain, but the waterproof kept the wind out. Whenever he remembered the farmhouse from his childhood it was windy – the fertilizer bags blowing about in the yard, blustery on the track up to the sheep hills, in the big field that had been the family's mainstay ever since his father had cleared the rocks from it, in the potato field. Wind, more than rain or frost, characterized the place, not that there wasn't a lot of rain too. But who'd mind the rain? his father used to say.

The heifers didn't need seeing to, as he had known they wouldn't. They stood, miserably crouched in against the wall of a fallen barn, mud that the wind had dried hanging from them. His father had taken off the roof when one of the other walls had collapsed, needing the corrugated iron for somewhere else. He'd left the standing wall for the purpose the heifers put it to now.

Paulie, too, stood in the shelter of the wall, the puddles at his feet not yet blown dry, as the mud had on the animals. He remembered the red roof lifted down, piece by piece,

Kevin waiting below to receive it, Aidan wrenching out the bolts. He had backed the tractor, easing the trailer close to where they were. 'What's he want it for?' he'd asked Kevin, and Kevin said the corrugated iron would be used for filling the gaps in the hedges.

Slowly, Paulie walked back the way he had come. 'D'you think of coming back?' Aidan had said, saying it in the yard when they were alone. Paulie had known it would be said and had guessed it would be Aidan who'd say it, Aidan being the oldest. 'I'm only mentioning it,' Aidan had said. 'I'm only touching on it.'

*

Blowing at the turf with the wheel-bellows, she watched the glow spread, sparks rising and falling away. It hadn't been the time to make arrangements or even to talk about them. Nothing could have been more out of place, and she was glad they realized that. Kevin had had a word with Hartigan after the funeral, something temporary fixed up, she could tell from the gestures.

They'd write. Frances had said she would, and Aidan had. Sharon would write for Kevin, as she always did. Mena would. Wherever it was they stopped to say good-bye to one another they'd talk about it and later on they'd write.

'Sit down, Paulie, sit down,' she said when her son came in, bringing the cold with him.

She said again that Father Kinally had done it beautifully. She'd said so yesterday to her daughters in the car, she'd said it to Kevin and to Aidan this morning. Paulie would have heard, yet you'd want to repeat it. You felt the better for it.

'Ah, he did,' Paulie said. 'He did of course.'

He'd taken over. She could feel he'd taken over, the way he'd gone out to see were the heifers all right, the way it was he who remembered, last evening and this morning, that there was the bit of milking to do, that he'd done it without a word. She watched him ease off the gum boots and set them down by the door. He hung the waterproof on the door hook that was there for it and came to the fire in his socks, with his shoes in one hand. She turned away so that he wouldn't notice she'd been reminded of his father coming into the kitchen also.

'Aren't the heifers looking good?' she said.

'Oh, they are, they are.'

'He was pleased with them this year.'

'They're not bad, all right.'

'Nothing's fetching at the minute, all the same.'

He nodded. He naturally would know times were bad, neither sheep nor cattle fetching what they were a year ago, everything gone quiet, the way you'd never have believed it.

'We're in for the night so,' she said.

'We are.'

She washed the eggs Mena had collected earlier, brushing off the marks on them, then wiped the shells clean before she piled them in the bowl. The eggs would keep them going, with the rashers left over and half a saucepan of stew in the fridge. 'You've enough for an army!' Kevin had said, looking into the deep-freeze, and she reminded him you had to have enough in case the weather came in bad.

'What'd we do without it?' she said now, mentioning the deep-freeze. They'd had half a pig from the Caslins, only a portion of the belly used up so far. 'And mutton till Dooms-day,' she said.

'How're they these days, the Caslins? I didn't notice Maureen at the funeral.'

'Maureen married a man in Tralee. She's there since.'

'Who's the man?'

'He's in a shoe shop.'

They could have gone to the wedding only it had been a period of the year when you wouldn't want to spare the time. The Hartigans had gone. They'd have taken her but she'd said no.

'Hartigan came back drunk, you should have seen the cut of him! And herself with a frost on her that would have quenched the fire!'

'He's driving down in the morning. He'll pick me up.'

Rashers and black pudding and fried bread were ready on the pan. She cracked two eggs into the fat, turned them when they were ready because he liked them turned. When she placed the plate in front of him he took a mouthful of tea before he ate anything. He said:

'You couldn't manage. No way.'

'It wasn't a time to talk about it, Paulie.'

'I'll come back.'

He began to eat, the yolk of the eggs spreading yellow on the plate. He left the black pudding and the crisp fat of the bacon until last. He'd always done that.

'Hartigan'd still come down. I'm all right on the bit of

234

milking. I'm all right on most things. The Caslins would come up.'

'You couldn't live like that.'

'They're neighbours, Paulie. They got help from himself if they wanted it. I looked over and saw Kevin having a word with Hartigan in the graveyard. It won't be something for nothing, not with Hartigan. Kevin'll tell me later.'

'You'd be dependent.'

'You have your own life, Paulie.'

'You have what there is.'

He ate for several minutes in silence, then he finished the tea that had been poured for him.

'I'd have to give in notice. I'd have to work the notice out. A month.'

'Think it over before you'll do anything, Paulie.'

*

Paulie harboured no resentment, not being a person who easily did: going back to the farmhouse was not the end of the world. The end of the world had been to hear, in Meagher's back bar, that life on a farm did not attract Patsy Finucane.

As soon as he'd mentioned marriage that day he knew he shouldn't have. Patsy Finucane had taken fright like a little young greyhound would. She'd hardly heard him when he said, not knowing what else to say, 'Ah well, no matter.' It was a nervousness mixed in with the stout that had caused him to make the suggestion, and as soon as he had there was no regaining her: before she looked away that was there in her soft grey eyes. 'I won't go back so,' he'd said, making matters worse. 'I won't go back without you.'

When they sat again in Meagher's back bar after the funeral Paulie tried to put things right; he tried to begin again, but it wasn't any good. During the third week of his working out his notice Patsy Finucane began to go out with a clerk from the post office.

*

In the yard she threw down grains for the hens and re-membered doing it for the first time, apprehensive then about what she'd married into. Nor had her apprehension been misplaced: more than she'd imagined, her position in the household was one of obedience and humility, and sometimes what was said, or incidents that occurred, left a sting that in private drew tears from her. Yet time, simply in passing, transformed what seemed to be immutable. Old age enfeebled on the one hand; on the other, motherhood nur-tured confidence. In the farmhouse, roles were reversed.

She didn't want distress like that for any wife Paulie would eventually bring to the kitchen and the house. She would make it easier, taking a back seat from the start and be glad to do so. It was only a pity that Maureen Caslin had married the shoe-shop man, for Maureen Caslin would have suited him well. There were the sisters, of course.

During the weeks that followed Paulie's departure, the anticipated letters came from Mena and Frances and from her daughter-in-law Sharon on behalf of Kevin, and from Aidan. The accumulated content was simple, the unstated expectation stated at last, four times over in different hand-writing. Aidan said he and Paulie had had a talk about it. *You are good to think of me,* she wrote back, four times also.

Hartigan continued to come down regularly and a couple of times his sister accompanied him, sitting in the kitchen while he saw to any heavy work in the yard. 'Would Mena have room for you?' she enquired on one of these occasions, appearing to forget that Paulie was due to return when he'd worked out his notice. Miss Hartigan always brought sultana bread when she came and they had it with butter on it. 'I only mentioned Mena,' she said, 'in case Paulie wouldn't be keen to come back. I was thinking he maybe wouldn't.'

'Why's that, Miss Hartigan?'

'It's bachelors that's in the hills now. Like himself,' Miss Hartigan added, jerking her bony head in the direction of the yard, where her brother was up on a ladder, fixing a gutter support.

'Paulie's not married either, though.'

'That's what I'm saying to you. What I'm saying is would he want to stop that way?'

Miss Hartigan's features were enriched by a keenness to say more, to inform and explain, to dispel the bewilderment she had caused. She did so after a pause, politely reaching for a slice of sultana bread. It might not have been noticed that these days the bachelors of the hills found it difficult to attract a wife to the modest farms they inherited.

'Excuse me for mentioning it,' Miss Hartigan apologized before she left.

*

It was true, and it had been noticed and often remarked upon. Hartigan himself, twenty years ago, was maybe the first of the hill bachelors: by now you could count them – lone men, some of them kept company by a mother or a sister – on the slopes of Coumpeebra, on Slievenacoush, on Knockrea, on Luirc, on Clydagh.

She didn't remember putting all that from her mind when Paulie had said he would come back, but perhaps she had. She tried not to think about it, comforting herself that what had been said, and the tone of Miss Hartigan's voice, had more to do with Miss Hartigan and her brother than with the future in a neighbouring farmhouse. Nor did it necessarily need to be that what had already happened would continue to happen. The Hartigans' stretch of land was worse by a long way than the land lower down on the hill; no better than the side of Slievenacoush, or Clydagh or Coumpeebra. You did the best you could, you hoped for warm summers. Paulie was a good-looking, decent boy; there was no reason at all why he wouldn't bring up a family here as his father had.

'There's two suitcases left down with the Caslins,' he said when he walked in one Saturday afternoon. 'When I get the car started I'll go down for them.'

They didn't embrace; there'd never been much of that in the family. He sat down and she made tea and put the pan on. He told her about the journey, how a woman had been singing on the first of the two buses, how he'd fallen asleep on the second. He was serious the way he told things, his expression intent, sometimes not smiling much. He'd always been like that.

'Hartigan started the car a while back,' she said, 'to make sure it was in form.'

'And it was? All right?'

'Oh, it was, it was.'

'I'll take a look at it later.'

He settled in easily, and she realized as he did so that she had never known him well. He had been lost to her in the family, his shadowy place in it influenced by his father's lack of interest in him. She had never protested about that, only occasionally whispering a surreptitious word or two of comfort. It was fitting in a way that a twist of fate had made him his father's inheritor.

As if he had never been away, he went about his daily tasks knowledgeably and efficiently. He had forgotten nothing – about the winter feed for the heifers, about the work around the yard or where the fences might give way on the hills or how often to go up there after the sheep, about keeping the tractor right. It seemed, which she had not suspected before, that while his presence was so often overlooked he had watched his father at work more conscientiously than his brothers had. 'He'd be proud of you these days,' she said once, but Paulie did not acknowledge that and she resisted making the remark again. The big field, which had been his father's pride, became his. There was another strip to the south of it that could be cleared and reclaimed, he said, and he took her out to show her where he would run the new wall. They stood in the sunshine on a warm June morning while he pointed and talked about it, the two sheepdogs obedient by him. He was as good with them as his father ever had been.

He drove her, as his father had, every three weeks down to Drunbeg, since she had never learned to drive herself. His father used to wait in the car park of Conlon's Supermarket while she shopped, but Paulie always went in with her. He pushed the trolley and sometimes she gave him a list and he added items from the shelves. 'Would we go and see that?' he suggested one time when they were passing the Two-Screen Rialto, which used to be just the Picture House before it was given a face-lift. She wouldn't be bothered, she said. She'd never been inside the cinema, either in the old days or since it had become a two-screen; the television was enough for her. 'Wouldn't you take one of the Caslin girls?' she said.

He took the older of them, Aileen, and often after that he drove down in the evenings to sit with her in the Master McGrath. The relationship came to an end when Aileen announced that her sister in Tralee had heard of a vacancy in a newsagent and confectioner's, that she'd been to Tralee herself to be looked over and in fact had been offered the position.

'And did you know she had intentions that way?' Paulie's mother asked him when she heard, and he said he had, in a way. He didn't seem put about, although she had assumed herself that by the look of things Aileen Caslin – stolid and on the slow side – would be the wife who'd come to the farmhouse, since her sister Maureen was no longer available. Paulie didn't talk about it, but quite soon after Aileen's departure he began to take an interest in a girl at one of the pay-outs in Conlon's.

'Wouldn't you bring Maeve out one Sunday?' his mother suggested when the friendship had advanced, when there'd been visits to the two-screen and evenings spent together drinking, as there'd been with Aileen Caslin. Maeve was a fair bit livelier than Aileen; he could do worse.

But Maeve never came to the farmhouse. In Conlon's Paulie took to steering the trolley to one of the other pay-outs even when the queue at hers was shorter. His mother didn't ask why. He had his own life, she kept reminding herself; he had his privacy, and why shouldn't he? 'Isn't he the good boy to you?' Father Kinally remarked one Sunday after Mass when Paulie was turning the car. 'Isn't it grand the way it's turned out for you?'

She knew it was and gratefully gave thanks for it. Being more energetic than his father had been at the end, Paulie worked a longer day, far into the evening when it was light enough.

'I don't know did I ever speak a word to her,' she said when he began to go out with the remaining Caslin daughter. Sensible, she looked.

*

'Ah, sure, anything,' the youngest of the three Caslin girls always said when Paulie told her what films were on and asked which she'd like to see. When the lights went down he waited a bit before he put an arm around her, as he always had with her sisters and with Maeve. He hadn't been able to wait with Patsy Finucane.

The sensible look that Paulie's mother had noted in Annie

Caslin was expressed in a matter-of-fact manner. Sentiment played little part in her stalwart, steady nature. She was the tallest and in a general way the biggest of the three Caslin girls, with black hair that she curled and distinctive features that challenged one another for dominance – the slightly large nose, the wide mouth, the unblinking gaze. Paulie took her out half a dozen times before she confessed that what she wanted to do was to live in a town. She'd had the roadside Master McGrath, she said; she'd had serving petrol at the pumps. 'God, I don't know how you'd stand it up in the bogs,' she said before Paulie had a chance to ask her if she'd be interested in coming up to the farmhouse. Even Drunbeg would do her, she said, and got work six months later in the fertilizer factory.

Paulie asked other girls to go out with him, but by then it had become known that what he was after was marriage. One after another, they made excuses, a fact that Hartigan was aware of when he pulled up the Toyota one morning beside a gateway where Paulie was driving in posts. He didn't say anything, but often Hartigan didn't.

'Will it rain, Mr Hartigan?' Paulie asked him.

'The first time I saw your mammy,' Hartigan said, rejecting a discussion about the weather, 'she was stretching out sheets on the bushes. Six years of age I was, out after a hare.'

'A while ago, all right.'

'Amn't I saying it to you?'

Not understanding the conversation, Paulie vaguely shook his head. He struck the post he was easing into the ground another blow. Hartigan said:

'I'd take the big field off you.'

'Ah no, no.'

That was why he had stopped. It might even have been that he'd driven down specially when he heard the thud of the sledgehammer on the posts, saying to himself that it was a good time for a conversation.

'I wouldn't want to sell the field, Mr Hartigan.'

'But wouldn't you do well all the same if you did? Is it a life at all for a young fellow?'

Paulie didn't say anything. He felt the post to see if it was steady yet. He struck it again, three times before he was satisfied.

'You need a bit of company, boy,' Hartigan said before he backed into the gateway and drove up the hill again.

*

What she had succeeded in keeping at bay since Miss Hartigan had spoken of it was no longer possible to evade. When Paulie told her about Patsy Finucane she was pleased that he did, glad that he didn't keep it to himself. She knew about everything else: it was all of a piece that Hartigan was trying to get the land cheap by taking advantage of the same circumstances that had left him a bachelor himself. Who could blame him? she said to herself, but even so she wondered if Paulie – so agreeable and good-hearted – would become like that in his time; if he'd become hard, as his father had been, and as grasping as Hartigan.

'I'll go to Mena,' she said. 'There's room there.'

'Ah, there isn't.'

'They'd fit me in.'

'It's here there's room.'

'You want to be married, Paulie. Any man does.'

'He'd take a day shifting a boulder with the tractor. He'd put a ditch through the marsh to gain another half yard. He never minded how long a thing took.'

'It's now we're talking about, Paulie.'

'There'd be sheep in this house within a twelvemonth if Hartigan had it, the doors taken off and made use of, and the next thing is the wind'd be shifting the slates. There'd be grazing taken out of the big field until there wasn't a blade of grass left standing. The marsh'd come in again. No one'd lift a finger.'

'You didn't know what you were coming back to.'

'Ah, I did. I did.'

Obligingly, he lied. You'd say to yourself he was easygoing. When he'd told her about the Finucane girl he'd said it was the way things were. No matter, he'd said. Often you'd forget he wasn't easygoing at all; often she did.

'There's no need, Paulie.'

'There is.'

He said it quietly, the two words hanging there after he had spoken, and she realized that although it was her widowhood that had brought him back it wasn't her widowhood that made him now insist he must remain. She could argue for ever and he would not go now.

'You're good, Paulie,' she said, since there was nothing else left to say.

He shook his head, his dark hair flopping from side to side. 'Arrah, no.'

'You are. You are, Paulie.'

When her own death came, her other children would return, again all at the same time. The coffin would be carried down the steep stairs, out into the van in the yard, and the funeral would go through the streets of Drunbeg, and the next day there'd be the Mass. They'd go away then, leaving Paulie in the farmhouse.

'Wait till I show you,' he said, and he took her out to where he was draining another half yard. He showed her how he was doing it. He showed her the temporary wall he had put up, sheets of red corrugated that had come from the old shed years ago.

'That's great,' she said. 'Great, Paulie.'

A mist was coming in off the hills, soft and gentle, the clouds darkening above it. The high edge of Slievenacoush was lost. Somewhere over the boglands a curlew cried.

'Go in out of the drizzle,' he said, when they had stood there for a few minutes.

'Don't stay out long yourself, Paulie.'

Guilt was misplaced, goodness hardly came into it. Her widowing and the mood of a capricious time were not of consequence, no more than a flicker in a scheme of things that had always been there. Enduring, unchanging, the hills had waited for him, claiming one of their own.